"THE MAZES OF SOME MYSTIC AND INTRICATE MEASURE."

*New Border Tales.*]

# THE NEW

# BORDER TALES

BY

SIR GEORGE DOUGLAS, BART.,

AUTHOR OF "THE FIRESIDE TRAGEDY."

THE WALTER SCOTT PUBLISHING CO., LTD.

LONDON AND NEWCASTLE-ON-TYNE.

NEW YORK: 3 EAST 14TH STREET.

THE WALTER SCOTT PUBLISHING CO., LTD., NEWCASTLE-ON-TYNE.

12-04

## Dedication.

---

### To

### GEORGE LANDELS,

*Gamekeeper,*

*Springwood Park.*

*My Dear George,*

      *I could not rightly associate any name but yours with my own on the first page of this book of tales; for are not several of the tales yours as much as, if not more than, mine? When a tradition was unearthed, or a story conceived, did we not always talk it over together? You gave to each story, when it was written down, a first patient hearing; and, during the pleasant year whilst the little book has been writing, in whose society have I spent so much time as in yours?   Did not we visit in company Swindon Wood and Ellen's Tree, and the scenes of Willie Wastle's treasure-trove, and of Rob Scott's sudden fit of madness?   To the fraternal wrestling-bout— tradition failing us—we assigned a locality, not far removed from the lone memorials on the hill. Wading, angle in hand, in the shallow streams of Teviot; wandering on Sundays on those well-beloved sylvan banks; watching beside a rabbit-burrow, by some tree-root in the grass-parks, when your ferret, Nean, persistently "lay in"; tramping over many a sea of turnips, coloured like Ocean and not much less wet; seated in the cabin by the pheasant-rearing ground in summer, or as we worked together twisting wire for snares upon a winter's night, we gave these stories their shape. Too often, when the day was over, the game-bag would be light, the creel empty—your despair; but, despite apparent failure, I was well content, for seldom or never did I come in at night otherwise than enriched—it might be by some new racy word, or phrase, of our dear Border language, it might be by some naïve and genial trait of peasant manners, or by the limb or the torso of a tradition disin-*

*terred. For the two of us, then, these stories have their associations. But will they, by others to whom we are unknown, be deemed worthy of association with the name of that beloved and beauteous tract of earth into which so many hearts —and, among them, one of the greatest of all human hearts—have struck their roots so deeply? That is, indeed, a very different matter. However, that, also, time will show. Meanwhile, my dear George, accept the stories—imperfect as they are, and believe me to remain, in absence,*

*Ever your attached Friend and Master,*

*GEORGE DOUGLAS.*

Several of the subjects of these stories are traditional. A passage in *The Brither Stanes* will be
recognised as a prose transcript from one of the old
ballads.

# CONTENTS.

———◦●◦———

# THE NEW BORDER TALES.

## THE CHIEF MOURNER.

AT a late hour of the night, two friends sat together over a dying fire.

"I have given you my experience of the supernatural," said the first; "now, let me have yours."

The other shook his head.

"I have none to give." And, after a pause, he continued, "You forget, S., that I am the child of a scientific age. For me, belief has one basis, and one alone—the evidence of the senses. I believe in what I can see, touch, hear; and anything else in which I am to believe must be deduced from this by a process of reasoning which I can test or check. Now, I have never seen a ghost; *ergo* I don't believe in ghosts."

"And you discredit the evidence of those who say they have?"

1

"Not in the sense you mean—I should be extremely sorry to doubt the word of a friend; and more than one of my friends have, like yourself, at least seen something of a ghostly nature. But, tho' my friends don't tell fibs, I think it is quite possible that they may make mistakes— that they may imagine a ghost where in reality ghost is none. And my conclusion is that all ghosts which are not the creations of simple fiction, exaggeration, or inaccuracy, may be explained by one out of three kinds of causes. These causes are: first, natural phenomena— such as shadows, a patch of white light, an accidental fantastic arrangement of light and shade ; secondly, the morbid symptoms of brain- or nerve-sickness—hallucinations, delusions, and the like ; and, thirdly, coincidences—those extraordinary concatenations of circumstance which have given rise to the proverb that truth is stranger than fiction : these things, I say, *plus* a mistaken attribution of the relation of cause and effect."

"Ah!—well, at the present moment, my dear D., I could wish that you had not been the 'child of a scientific age.' However, though you have yourself had no personal experience of the supernatural, and don't believe in it, are there no ghost-stories connected with your house? One would think that there ought to be."

"There is one such story ; and, to tell you the

truth, it is one which I have hitherto taken some trouble to keep from becoming public property. For, notwithstanding that the age in which we live is scientific, thought has not yet "come down among the crowd." In other words, the light shed by science has not yet penetrated to the world below stairs. And were my story to become known in the house, it might give rise to trouble among the maid-servants."

"Delightful! To think that you have such a story and never yet have mentioned it to me! Pray let me hear it at once."

"If you wish it, certainly. My story, then, let me premise, is one which is concerned with what, in the jargon of the ghost-seeing world, is called, I believe, specifically, a *warning*."

"An excellent variety of the ghost-story!"

"Well, my authority for what I am going to tell you is my aunt, Miss Caroline D., whom you have met. She, as you know, is in a way of her own a sort of antiquarian. Old customs, old stories, old-world odds and ends of every kind— all such worn-out waifs are her delight. But her speciality is old family history, and in particular the history of our own family. Well, these fads, as you must know, are no recent development in her character, but have characterised her from girlhood; at which period of her life she used, I believe, to find great pleasure in the society of a certain Mr. Dalziel, a Writer to the Signet, who had been our family lawyer, who was at that time an old man and able to gratify her appetite for gossip about the dead and gone. The narrative which I am about to relate she received from this Dalziel's lips and communicated to me. Dalziel was an actor in the events described; so that you see that the story now comes to yourself only (so to put it) at third-hand. Dalziel was assuredly no romancer; my aunt Caroline, though by no means without her foibles, has, I verily believe, too much respect for the past to seek to colour history; and, as for myself, a scientific training, whatever may be its drawbacks, has certainly, as I think you will allow, the advantage of cultivating accuracy. So that I think you may reckon upon hearing what took place described, without loss or addition, pretty much as it occurred.

"My great-grandfather, Sir George D.—for reasons into which I need not enter—lived for many years with his family on the Continent, and during their absence this house was kept shut up. At length, however, he found himself at liberty to return and take up his abode here; which, accompanied by his wife and an only daughter, he proceeded to do. Sir George may be supposed to have been very glad to be at home again; and by way of celebrating his return, he invited a small party of friends and relations, whom he had not seen for some time, to meet him at Silverwood, to spend a few days in renewing acquaintance, and in enjoying those natural beauties of the place which had remained so long unadmired.     Among the guests thus assembled were the afore-mentioned Mr. Dalziel —then a youngish man, occupying a subordinate position—who was in attendance to transact business and supply information, and a certain maiden lady, a ' Scotch cousin ' of the family, whose whalebone constitution, ready tongue, and caustic raillery, together with an inexhaustible fund of stories, which were alternately broadly humorous and terrifying, made her, notwith-standing advanced age and broken fortunes, still a notable person in the Scotch society of her day. (It will interest you, as a literary man, to know that she is one of the old ladies referred to, though her name is not given, in the late Dean Ramsay's well-known book of old Scotch traits and stories.)   Sir George, as I have been told, was always very kind to this old lady, and showed her great attention—partly, no doubt, because she was a poor relation, but also because he really liked her.   But there were plenty of other people, who—being of less kindly nature, or, perhaps, because, having been trained in a more modern school, they were unable to appreciate her—laughed at the old woman (behind her back, as you may be very sure) and thought her a nuisance.  Her name was Miss

Euphame Pirie, and my great-grandfather always spoke of her and addressed her as his 'Aunt Euphame,' though she did not in reality stand in that relationship to him. Besides the above, the party numbered some four or five others, whose names will either be mentioned later on, or need not be mentioned at all.

"Sir George, as I have already indicated, was in high spirits at finding himself at home once more, with the prospect of remaining there. He was a born country-gentleman, with two tastes —sport and the management of an estate—which, poor man, he was fated not to gratify. Lady D. did not share his elation. From all I have ever heard of my great-grandmother, I should judge her to have been an elegant woman, of no great depth of character. Certainly she preferred the polished society and the round of amusements of a foreign city to life in a Scotch country house. The state of mind, again, of Miss D.— or Johnina, as she had been christened in compliment to Lord John S., an old friend and kinsman of her father's—partook both of Sir George's elation and of her mother's *ennui*. In her artificial tastes, which had been fostered by a Parisian education, in the shallowness of her nature, evinced by her love of pleasure, change, and of society, I judge her to have been her mother's daughter—and, as such, more fitted for a town life than for the country. On the other hand,

she was a mere girl—not more than seventeen
years old—and novelty itself was a source of the
keenest pleasure to her.  You have seen Johnina's
portrait, painted in miniature by Cosway.  It is
the finest in my collection.  In her rose-leaf
complexion, her large and swimming eyes of
sky-blue, in the ethereal nature and the trembling sensibility expressed in her countenance,
that great artist found a subject worthy of his
exquisite skill.  And I remember that, long ago,
when I used to read of 'sylph-like forms,' in old-
fashioned novels, I always thought of this portrait
of Johnina.  But I think it must have been a little
idealised.  I don't wish to judge the girl harshly;
but I gather from the story which I am about to
tell you (which, indeed, embodies all that I know
concerning her), that, if there was something of
the angel in Johnina's appearance, there was
something of the elf in her disposition.  A very
small example may serve to illustrate what
I mean.  She spent the first morning after
her return home—which was also (had she but
known it) the most important in her life—as was
natural enough, in eager exploration of the house
and its precincts.  She had left Silverwood at an
early age; yet some recollections, however slight,
of days of infancy passed there must still have
lingered in her mind.  With most of us such
recollections are apt to be regarded as precious
spiritual possessions, sanctifying and endearing,

though it were mean and homely, the abode about which they cling. But with Miss D. it was otherwise. I will not take it upon me to say that she lacked heart or reverence altogether; all I know is that her first criticisms upon this old house are said to have been liberal and trenchant, whilst she derived a good deal of food for mirth from 'quizzing' its furniture and other contents. I have also been informed that, on the very evening of their arrival, she and her mother set their brains to work to design sweeping alterations—or, as they called them, improvements— to be carried out here. So sweeping, indeed, were the changes proposed, that, had there been a presiding genius or household-spirit in the place, the very mention of them might have been enough to rouse him from his dusky lair and from his age-long lethargy, to make one final appearance, like Barbarossa, long after his date was closed, and so, by a monstrous interference with the course of nature, emphatically protest against, or forbid, the purposed desecration. However, for reasons which you will presently understand, the proposed alterations were not carried out.

"Among the assembled guests there is still one who remains to be specified. He was a young gentleman of the neighbourhood, Beaumont by name. Whilst completing his education in the approved manner of the day, by performing the 'grand tour,' he had spent some time with the D.'s upon the Continent, with the result that he was now a suitor for Johnina's hand. His family was a good one; he was his own master, and the owner of a considerable landed estate; and he further bore the character of being an amiable and sensible young fellow, and was sincerely attached to Miss D. Sir George liked him, and would have sanctioned an engagement; and even her ladyship, generally so indifferent and hard to please, had expressed herself favourably towards him. But Miss Johnina, the principal party concerned, was more difficult to come to terms with. Flighty, mercurial, of a strangely nervous temperament, never knowing her own mind, or knowing it but to change it, Miss D. united the attributes of the spoiled and precocious child with those of the ideal mistress. The result was that, to all appearance, she played fast and loose with her lover, keeping him dangling at her heels whilst she occasionally encouraged other admirers, and no one in the world could say whether she intended finally to accept him or not. Beaumont's steadiness and staying-power were, however, greatly in his favour, and at the time of which I speak it seemed not improbable that he might gain the day. As regards Johnina, in all probability the surest method for precipitating matters would have been to set strong, and, if possible, authoritative, persuasions to work in the direction which was *not* desired.   But Sir George and his wife habitually indulged their daughter, allowing her to have her own way in all matters where her own interest was concerned, so that she felt that she was free to act in this matter entirely as she chose.

"Well, on the day following the return of the family, the party assembled in the dining-room about noon, to partake of *déjeuner à la fourchette.*   It did not suit my great-grandmother to put in an appearance very early in the day, and she had determined to keep to Continental hours at Silverwood.   Sir George—he must have been rather a fine old fellow, to judge from Raeburn's portrait of him—seated at the head of his table once more, a king in his castle, was extolling, as I have been told, the glories of a country gentleman's life.   (He had not as yet enjoyed them for full four-and-twenty hours, so that I, his degenerate descendant, born into an age of bad times, reduced rents, and dissatisfied tenantry, can at this distance of time forgive him.)

"'Why, I had rather any day be the Duke of B. than one of your petty German princes or potentates!   The Duke's income is larger than their revenue; his estate is as large as their principality.   His power, in all that makes power worth having, is as great as theirs; and he is not plagued with the intolerable tedium of a Court and perpetual etiquette.'

"Dalziel, the person addressed, confined himself to politely murmuring assent. If accounts may be trusted, he appears to have been an ideal man of business—that is, in all matters where business was not concerned, an entirely characterless person. As he has been described to me, his every word, opinion, act, had the colourlessness of absolute propriety. Imagine a man who should never surprise, never shock, never even disappoint!

"Miss Euphame now inquired how Johnina came to be absent.

"'She is late, I suppose,' murmured Lady D. 'In fact, it is seldom she is otherwise.'

"'You ought not to allow her to be late. In my young days, if one of us came late to a meal she went without it. But it is true that in those days the old heads governed the young. Now, it seems to be the other way about.'

"It was summer-time. The day was warm and bright, and a somewhat extended expedition, to visit the grounds, had been planned for the afternoon. This would make a punctual start desirable; so that, as the moments passed and still Johnina did not appear, her father rose from his seat to go and look for her.

"'Allow me to go,' said Beaumont, rising also.

"But at this moment an incident occurred which violently turned the current of their thoughts:—that most dreadful of all sounds, the shriek of a human creature in ghastly terror or in deadly pain, rang through the house and tore their ears. It came from one of the upper floors, but it so happened that doors had been left open to remove a smell of paint, and thus it pealed out clear and awful as if uttered close at hand. Of course the voice was not recognisable; but old Mr. Dalziel, when he used to tell my aunt the story, always laid particular stress on the singularly terrifying quality of the cry.

"With one accord all started to their feet, and in less than a moment every man had rushed from the room and was flying up the stairs in the direction whence the sound proceeded. Dalziel, who had been seated nearest to the door, came first, and when he reached the angle of the staircase, there upon the landing in front of him, looking as if a breath would blow her away, stood the frail figure of Johnina. She was clothed in white muslin, on account of the heat; but, as Dalziel always declared, her dress, when he first caught sight of her, was not whiter than her countenance, and she was shaking like an aspen leaf.

"'Miss Johnina!' exclaimed the breathless lawyer, 'Great heavens! what has happened?'

"But, to the astonishment, and, as I need not

add, to the great relief of everybody, by one of the instantaneous transitions which were such a perplexing feature in her temperament, Johnina was now discovered to be laughing. So swift, indeed, was the change, that Dalziel alone, as he averred, was a witness of the terror of the one moment—those who were a step or two behind him on the stairs seeing only the merriment of the next.

"And now, indeed, Miss Johnina seemed almost as much overcome by the one emotion as it had been feared that she had before been by the other. Pressing one hand upon her side, she leaned back against the door-jamb in a fit of uncontrollable mirth.

"'Oh dear, oh dear!' she exclaimed, when at last she was able to speak, 'I protest that I shall die of laughing!'

"This was strange. Was the girl's behaviour genuine? was the question which Dalziel asked himself; or was she—ashamed of her former passion of fear, and afraid of being laughed at (about which she was indeed always particularly sensitive)—now trying to pass off something as a joke which had indeed been deadly earnest? Inexperienced in the young lady's April nature, the lawyer was perplexed.

"The party now returned to the dining-room; and Johnina, being interrogated as to the cause of her alarming cry, revealed what follows.—In the hope of lighting upon something pretty and to her taste, she had been occupied in ransacking a long-closed cupboard in a remote attic of the house, of the key of which she had somehow managed to possess herself. She had heard the lunch-bell ring; but, led on from treasure to treasure, had disregarded its summons. At last the recollection of the afternoon's expedition had darted through her giddy head; and, ever ready to leave the present for the future pleasure, she had started up to come downstairs. But, as she rose from her kneeling posture in front of the engrossing cupboard, she had suddenly become aware of the disquieting fact that she was not alone. And the nature and garb of the intruder were not such as to inspire confidence. The figure of an elderly man of austere aspect, dressed in the intensely funereal garb affected by a Scotchman of the middle class when he attends a funeral, was standing in the half-light just outside the attic doorway, his eyes being fixed upon her. Amazed at finding herself not only not alone (as she had fully believed herself to be), but attended, or, as it seemed, watched, by a companion at once so startling and so mournful, so forbidding, ungainly, and extravagant, in the first moment of her surprise, Johnina had screamed aloud. Whereupon the mourner seemed to have glided silently through one of the open doors, and so

been lost to view; whilst the young girl had
fled like the wind toward the more frequented
parts of the house, reaching the landing where
she had been discovered from above at the same
moment as her friends had reached it from
below.

"Her momentary alarm seemed now, however, to have entirely passed away; and, indeed,
the above statement was not made without
several brief relapses into a somewhat hysterical
laughter, and when it was concluded, Miss D.
laughed long and loud.

"'A Scotchman bent upon enjoying himself—
ha, ha! That is what I saw. And as I had
never seen one before, only heard him described, no wonder that it alarmed me.'

"(I must observe that Lady D. and her
daughter had returned from their long residence
abroad primed with many gibes and sneers
against Scotchmen, whom they chose to represent as a nation who divided their time between
listening to interminable sermons and getting
drunk on whisky, only snatching an interval of
repose and relaxation on those congenial occasions when they buried a relation or a friend.)

"'Such a quizzical figure!' continued the
young lady, '*Mais je vous assure* . . . *fagoté
jusqu' aux yeux*—black frock, black breeches,
black gloves, white bands, and the most ample
"weepers." He must certainly have been the

Chief Mourner, whoever he was.  *Quel pays
ridicule!*  I vow that I shall die of laughing!'

"'Is one of the servants attending a funeral
to-day?' enquired her father of the butler.

"'Not that I know of, Sir George.'

"Johnina had flung herself forward over the
table in a new paroxysm of laughter.  Was
there not something factitious in this excess of
mirth provoked by such a cause?  Was there
not, at least, a suspicion that the young girl was
in a condition of over-excitement, and that she
was straining to laugh away the recollection of
some unpleasant impression which she had
received?

"During all this time Miss Euphame had
not spoken.  But an observer might have
noticed that her countenance was strangely
altered, and that as Johnina persisted in the
indulgence of her foolish hilarity, a dark cloud
was fast gathering on the old woman's brow.
But attention being centred elsewhere, she had
been for the moment unobserved; and when at
last she spoke, her discordant tones—like those
of a raven croaking ill-omen—produced an
effect upon her audience, which was different,
indeed, in character, but far less so in degree,
from that which had been produced by the
appalling sound of a few minutes before.

"'Have ye neither sense nor mense, woman,'
she cried aloud, relapsing, under the influence of

"HIS EYES BEING FIXED UPON HER."

New Border Tales.]

strong emotion, into a Doric yet more guttural than her habitual medium of expression—'Have ye neither sense nor mense, to demean yersel' that gait—for a' the warld like some puir dementit haverel? Bairn, let me tell ye that ye are nae better than a French fule, without heart's compassion for his fellow-man, nor respect for that which is abune man's comprehension!'

"Miss Euphame's tones were those of right-eously indignant reproach. Her deep eyes lightened, her strongly-marked features were transformed, and she wore, as she spoke, the aspect of a denouncing sibyl or prophetess. An awkward silence fell upon the company; for even the most light-minded person present (much as he might wish to do it) could scarcely in sincerity refer those deep tones of conviction to a mere freak of senile irritability. Johnina was wholly unaccustomed to be spoken to roughly, and her eyes in spite of her filled with tears, which her pride struggled vainly to conceal. At the same time it was quite plain that the feeling which had brought them there was no amiable compunction at having thought-lessly given offence, but a naughty resentment against her harsh reprover. She turned to her next neighbour, a young gentleman named Pringle, and in a voice which was by no means inaudible, though a little shaken by her sobs, pronounced the words:

**2**

" 'Old cat ! '

" Pringle with difficulty stifled his amusement; but fortunately it seemed that Miss Euphame's sense of hearing, dulled by age, had not allowed her to catch the words. She had withdrawn into herself once more, and now wore an air of profound and melancholy abstraction, to all appearance dead to what was taking place around her.

" The expediency of bringing the meal to as early a termination as possible was apparent to every one. Further supplies were declined, and in a few minutes Lady D. pushed back her chair and, followed by the other ladies, rose to leave the room.

"As they passed out at the door, Miss Euphame laid her hand on Johnina's waist, and employing a far softer voice than before, murmured not unkindly in her ear:

" 'Learn wisdom, learn wisdom, my dear! You have need of it, and your time may be short enough.'

" But either Miss D. had not yet forgiven her kinswoman's previous harshness, or else she did not relish the wrath-to-come character of the present good advice. She hastily shook off the old lady's arm, and moved huffily away, just like the spoiled child she was.

" After lingering behind for a few minutes, the men joined the ladies, and on Sir George's instigation various details of the plans for the

afternoon began to be debated.   No great eagerness to set out was at first displayed ; and, in
fact, it was discovered that there were to be
several seceders from the party.   Lady D.
excused herself upon the score of fatigue after
her journey.   Miss Euphame had disappeared,
having withdrawn to her own room, whence she
presently sent a message desiring that Sir George
would speak with her.   The baronet went away,
promising to return immediately ; but minute
followed minute, and still he did not reappear.
The party grew tired of waiting; conversation
languished ; and an atmosphere of fatigue and
depression began to weigh upon the little circle.
Any one among them would have given a handsome sum to have seen the proposed pleasure-
party abandoned, and to have been left to spend
the afternoon according to his own devices ; but
they were visitors in a friend's house, and politeness
hindered any one from taking the initiative with
a proposal to that effect.   Only Beaumont good-
naturedly exerted himself to make the best of
things ; and, to revive the flagging interest of
the party, proposed to take them on the water.
Johnina jumped at the idea, and the company
in general approved ; but at this moment Sir
George at length returned from his interview
with Miss Euphame, and after apologising for
having kept them waiting, somewhat curtly
vetoed the proposal.

"Of course Johnina protested vehemently. However, it was to no purpose; for she merely succeeded in eliciting from her father the information that he had given an undertaking to his old aunt (as he called her) that none of the party should go upon the water that day.

"'The old lady is nervous and fanciful,' he explained, with some degree of preoccupation in his manner. 'She has taken some fancy as to the danger of boating into her head, and nothing would satisfy her but that I should give her my word that none of us would attempt it to-day. As she made such a point of it, I thought it best to humour her; but I have also ascertained from the gardener that the Teviot is in half-flood, after yesterday's thunder-showers, so that in any case it would not have been prudent for us to have ventured upon it.'

"After this, of course no objection was raised by the visitors, though Miss Johnina still continued to murmur at having been baulked of her water-party. In the present state of the weather, as she maintained, there was no form of pleasure at all comparable to boating,—walking, riding, and driving, being each of them one more unendurable than the rest. It was inexpressibly stupid of Sir George to have bound himself by any undertaking to Miss Euphame, whose sole object, since she could not be happy herself, was to prevent others being so. Finally, she (Johnina) did not believe that the river was so much flooded as to make boating upon it in any degree unsafe or impracticable.

"It must be confessed that nobody paid much heed to the young lady's complaints and lamentations. Even the devoted Beaumont knew her ways too well for that; and, besides, he was of too sensible and sterling a character to seek to gain her favour by flattering her weaknesses. At last, it having been decided that walking was to be the method of their transit, the party began to move off.

"Now it happened that among those who remained behind was Mr. Dalziel. He was a bachelor, and not very fond of society. Perhaps he did not feel inclined for so long a walk as that proposed; perhaps he did not consider that his company was required. In any case, having now retired to his bedroom, he drew forth some documents from a private receptacle, and determined to enjoy his afternoon in his own way by devoting it to the accomplishment of some dry, legal task. When his work was done, as he said to himself, he would sally forth in the cool of the evening, with a satisfied conscience, and perhaps fall in with the walking-party on their way home.

"I have said that it was summer. The temperature was high, and the air, which had been only partially relieved by the storm of the day before, oppressive. It seemed that there would be more thunder to come. When Dalziel had sat for some time over his papers, he felt so drowsy that he determined to lie down for half-an-hour. Accordingly he drew down the blind, leaving the casement open, divested himself of his coat and boots, and lay down on the bed. (I may here point out that this part of the narrative, which is concerned with his own particular experience, was always, as might be expected, the most circumstantial.)

" In a few moments he was asleep. How long he slept he could not tell—it may have been an hour, it may have been only a few minutes; neither was he able to say whether his waking was natural or the result of some artificial cause. But, almost immediately after his senses had returned to him, and whilst his eyes were still closed, a startling incident occurred. Within a short distance of his ear, he distinctly heard a voice, which was unknown to him, repeat the following three sentences from the Liturgy of the Church of England :

" ' *Lord, have mercy upon us.*

" ' *Christ, have mercy upon us.*

" ' *Lord, have mercy upon us.*'

" The accents were those of the deepest tribu-lation, of an almost agonised supplication. When questioned in after years as to whether he were sure that he was not dreaming, he invariably

replied that he was ready to make oath in a court
of justice that he had been awake some moments
at the time when the voice was heard, and, further,
that the said voice was actual, and no mere
creation of his somnolent fancy.

"For the first moment his blood was curdled ;
but, quickly recovering himself, he started up
from the bed, more puzzled than alarmed, and
began to look about him. He was alone in the
room. He opened the door and looked out—the
passage was deserted. He glanced from the
window—there was no person in sight. Could
the sound have come from some adjoining room ?
Impossible—the walls at Silverwood, as he knew,
were too thick. Besides, was there any one in
the house who would be likely to put up such a
prayer, in such tones, at such an hour ? Deeply
impressed, and much perplexed, he lay down
once more to collect his thoughts.

"Strange as it may appear, he had not been
reclining long when he again fell asleep. His
second period of repose lasted probably considerably longer than the first, but was attended by no
remarkable occurrence. At last, as he lay in an
uneasy doze, he experienced a dim and confused
sense of hearing men running and shouting on
the banks of the river,—which (as you know) flows
not far from the house. Then he awoke to full
consciousness. It was late in the afternoon. The
sweet summer air, grown somewhat fresher with

the decline of day, gently lifted and let fall the window-blind, and the shadow of the house had begun to stretch far out upon the turf of the lawn below. Oppressed by a vague sense of impending misfortune, which he vainly sought to reason down, Dalziel arose and made his way downstairs. In the hall he was met by Lady D.

"'Mr. Dalziel,' she exclaimed, in tones of stronger emotion than any which the lawyer had heard her employ before, 'have you seen anything of the rest of the party? They should have been at home for tea more than an hour ago. I am afraid that something must have happened!'

"Dalziel, surprised to see her ladyship so much perturbed by what was apparently so slight a cause, endeavoured to reassure her, and spoke in tones of cheerfulness and security which in his heart (he knew not why) he was far from feeling.

"'Depend upon it, my lady, the beauty of the day has tempted them, tempted them and led them astray, so that they have prolonged their walk beyond what was at first proposed.'

"But at that very moment, as if to give the lie direct to his words, the sky became overcast —darkening the hall, which was lighted by a skylight—and the low mutter of distant, long-expected thunder at last made itself heard.

"Her ladyship glanced upward toward the

THE TEVIOT AT SILVERWOOD.

threatening heaven. 'You must go and meet
them at once, Dalziel. And pray carry a cloak
with you—Johnina takes cold easily, and is
unaccustomed to this treacherous climate.'

"When the lawyer left the house, the sky
overhead was overcast by a heavy cloud, beyond
the margin of which the beams of the sun still
penetrated with what seemed a preternatural
brightness. As he proceeded, the first few
swollen drops of the approaching rain-storm
fell.

"Taking his way through the shrubberies, he
made in the direction of the river. All of a
sudden the wind, which had lain still all day,
got up, and moaned, and lifted the leafage. It
began to grow dark, as though the twilight hour
were anticipated. Then, at the end of one of
the walks before him, Dalziel caught sight of a
figure flying fast in his direction. It was Sir
George, hatless, his grey elf-locks streaming in
the air. Without pausing in his swift career, he
passed close to the lawyer, with never a word or
sign of recognition. This was most unlike his
ordinary behaviour. 'I suppose he must be
hastening in to escape the rain,' surmised the
disingenuous Dalziel.

"He knew then, in his heart, that it was not
so; and a few moments more revealed the
nature of the catastrophe which had occurred.
Turning an angle in the walk which he was

following, he came full in view of that which
soon told him the worst. A singular procession
was advancing, at a melancholy pace, to meet
him. At the head of it, uncovered, his head
bowed, his hands clasped before him, in an
attitude of despair, walked Beaumont—than
whom, but an hour before, none had borne
himself more erect. Next came two of the
gardeners, who bore between them one of those
hand-barrows which are used in gardens for
transporting pot-plants. The wood of this
barrow was stained with moisture, and upon
it lay what seemed at first sight to be a heap
of white drapery—like clothes carried from a
bleaching-green or laundry—from among the
folds of which ran and dripped water. Behind,
with a strange, awe-struck, reverent air, came—
slowly, notwithstanding the on-coming storm—
young Pringle and two or three others. When
Dalziel saw this his heart sank; but his bewildered brain did not at once take in the situation.

"'Mr. Beaumont,' he cried, hurrying forward,
'what has happened?'

"Beaumont lifted a face which the lawyer
scarcely recognised, so strangely and sadly was
it altered. At the same moment the truth
flashed across him, and glancing hastily at the
barrow, he now too surely discerned in the mass
of drenched draperies the lifeless form of the
hapless Johnina.

"'How did it happen?'

"'God knows!  Will you go forward, Mr.
Dalziel, and assist Sir George to prepare her
poor mother?  I am not equal to the task.'

"The lawyer did as he was requested.  But
first he gently covered with the cloak which he
had brought with him for her use the cold limbs
and pale, still lineaments which were all that
now remained of the unfortunate Miss D.

"The circumstances of her death, at first
unknown to her friends, were in time brought to
light, and were as follows.  It may be remembered that, at setting out from the house,
Johnina had been in a somewhat pettish temper
—the result of her disappointment in the
matter of the water-party.  In immediate
attendance upon her, as she walked, were
Pringle and Beaumont.  At first she had
addressed herself to the task of persuading the
young men to disregard her father's expressed
wishes, and had brought all her feminine
artillery of wiles, blandishments, and affected
displeasure to bear upon them with this object.
But the men had stood their ground—Beaumont
being a young fellow of a very upright and
single-minded disposition, besides knowing well
with whom he had to deal, and Pringle being
guided by his example.  It was an unfortunate
circumstance, however, that the former allowed

himself to be entrapped into an admission that, apart from Sir George's injunction, he saw no reason (arising from the state of the river) why they should not venture upon it. Seeing that she was not to have her way, Johnina at last desisted from her importunities, and abruptly directed her efforts toward the entertainment of her companions by her conversation, in which she succeeded to admiration. All at once, however, she began to bewail an oversight by which she had come away from the house leaving a certain *vinaigrette*, which was indispensable, behind her. The willing Beaumont at once offered to return and fetch it—which, after some feigned reluctance, Miss D. permitted him to do. But no sooner was his back turned, than she once more began to assail Pringle with entreaties that he would give her an outing on the river. But Pringle, even when deprived of Beaumont's support, showed himself proof against all the ruses of her coquetry; and, after a time, the young couple walked onward again in silence. Presently they came to a place where the path divided—to re-unite, as they knew, at some distance further on. There the volatile Johnina proposed a race to the point of junction, Pringle being to take one of the branch paths, and she the other. The young man accordingly set off; but not so his companion. It was a characteristic of poor Miss D. that the considerable

degree of persistency with which she was
endowed was excited always, and alone, by
opposition.    She was determined not to be
baffled now.   No sooner, therefore, was Pringle
out of sight, than, instead of advancing in the
direction which he had taken, she must, it
seemed, have retraced her steps, making for the
spot on the river-bank where the boat was
moored.   Here she again came under observation.   An old man tending cattle among the
ruins of Roxburgh Castle, on the other side,
was the witness.   He saw her bend for some
moments over the moorings, and finally enter
the boat.   Fearing for her safety in the
flooded state of the river, he shouted to warn
her.   She must have heard him, for she waved
her little hand, no doubt in provocation, and
then proceeded to cast loose.   The river, as has
been said, was in half-flood,—that is, an able-
bodied man, accustomed to the use of oars, would
have incurred no great danger in managing a boat
upon it.   But Johnina was weak, and a town-bred
girl who knew nothing of boats or the like.   Indeed (so incredible was her folly!) it is doubtful
whether she had ever rowed before.   The boat
was carried out into the stream.   For a moment
or two she seemed to enjoy the motion, for she
let go the oars and clapped her hands.   But, a
second or two later, when the boat reached the
centre of the stream, the motion so increased as

to become terrifying in its rapidity and unsteadi-
ness.    Frightened out of her wits, the poor
child now seized the oars, to return, as she
imagined, to the shore.    But she was unskilful,
she had lost her head, and she only succeeded in
getting the boat 'broadside on' to the rapidly
racing billows, where in a few moments it was
overturned with herself beneath it.    So de-
liberate was the process of her unintentional
self-destruction, that I have been told that the
common people spoke of her, after her death, as
having been 'possessed,' or 'fey'—a term which
they apply, hereabouts, to a state of infatuation
in which a person walks deliberately, and with
his eyes open, to his own doom.

   "The cow-herd on the further bank, being
without a boat, was powerless to attempt render-
ing assistance, and it was long ere his distracted
cries were heard and the alarm was given.
Johnina's body, which had been lodged against
a point of land at a bend in the river some way
down, was recovered without difficulty.    But it
was brought ashore only that the discovery might
be made that life had been for some time extinct.

   "On the day following the funeral, Sir George
D. and his lady took their departure from Silverwood, never to return.    They are said never to
have recovered from the shock of their daughter's
terrible death; and the rest of their lives was
spent partly abroad, partly at Cheltenham.    This

house stood empty for some years, after which
it was made over as his residence to my grandfather, afterwards Sir John, who had at that time
just married a young wife, and retired from the
army. The youthful couple entirely dispelled
the gloom which had gathered round the place,
and themselves became celebrated for their
hospitality, and for the lavish style of living
which they kept up,—for which I, by the way,
am still paying. But before Sir George left
home, he communicated to Dalziel what had
passed between Miss Euphame and himself in the
long private interview which he had had with her,
after the French breakfast, on the forenoon of that
memorable day. His statement was to the effect
that, on entering her apartment, he had found
the old maiden-lady much disturbed in mind,
and labouring under a painful and characteristic
delusion. In one word, she believed that she
was fated to die that day ; and so firmly seated
was this belief, that, in the course of the interview, she even went so far as to give her kinsman,
who was to act as her executor, certain minute
testamentary instructions. Expostulated with
upon the groundlessness of her fears—for, though
advanced in years, her constitution, originally of
iron, was scarcely impaired—and questioned as
to how she had come to entertain them, the old
lady solemnly made this communication to my
great-grandfather.

"From time immemorial (as, no doubt, you have heard) some few old Scottish families have claimed to have their deaths foretold by what is called a 'Warning,' or harbinger. Well, among these families, as Miss Euphame now averred (though my great-grandfather does not seem to have known it), were the D.'s. The tradition of the D. apparition, as she went on to state, represented it as a figure of a forbidding aspect, attired in the old-fashioned garb worn by a chief mourner at a funeral. So that there was no room for doubt in the old lady's mind that the figure so unexpectedly seen by Johnina in the attic had been the family Warning. From this it was plain that a death in the family was about to occur; and though not herself the ghost-seer, being a member of the house of D., and certainly by many years the oldest of the party assembled in the house, Miss Euphame had made up her mind that the apparition had reference to her own demise, and, in short, that her hour was come. (I may observe in passing, that, as a matter of fact, she lived long after these events, dying, at last, in Edinburgh, at an age of upwards of ninety, and having retained the use of most of her faculties until very near the end.)

"After hearing what his elderly kinswoman had to say, Sir George had at first begun by pooh-poohing alike her superstitious tenets and the fears which they inspired. But finding speedily that, instead of reassuring her, this course merely produced the effect of disturbing her further, by rousing her to energetic protest, and at last to anger, he had adopted a soothing and conciliatory tone, judging it best to let her have her way, and had thus readily consented to give the promise which was required of him. (He was not himself a superstitious man, and it was only when he viewed it by the light of subsequent events that it occurred to him to see anything unusual in the fact of his daughter's having been confronted by a figure wearing mourning clothes. And by that time the opportunity for thoroughly, and with certainty, investigating the question of the figure's identity had gone by.) My great-grandfather, therefore, having done his best to calm the old gentlewoman, pressed her to take some rest, and saying to himself that decay had at last set in upon her faculties, left her to return to his guests. What followed you already know. It now only remains for me to add that, in the list of lives wrecked by Johnina's death, may be included that of Beaumont. Unreasonable as it seems, he was never able in his own mind to acquit himself of a certain share of blame and responsibility in that occurrence. This preyed upon him so that he grew depressed and melancholy. He never married ; and being the sole

3

representative of his race, his name, at his death, became extinct in the neighbourhood.

"Such is the Silverwood ghost-story, as I might call it—you may make of it what you please. For my own part, I must confess that, for a long time, I was rather inclined to believe in it—to believe in it as a ghost-story, of course, I mean. But this may have arisen from its being concerned with my own house and with members of my own family. Nevertheless it has certain points in its favour : the comparative nearness of the occurrence, the directness of the testimony, the 'dry light' of the chief witness,—the old lawyer's brain. However, by the expenditure of a little common sense, I think I have at last succeeded in resolving the whole fabric into the elements which are recognised by science. I will give you my explanation.

"As you will at once observe, it is only when they are taken *in combination* that the so-called supernatural incidents of the story are in any degree remarkable. In other words, it is one of those enigmas which may be resolved by the key of *coincidence*. Suppose Johnina to have seen a man in mourner's garb and thought he was a spectre, and nothing to have followed upon this, no more would have been thought about the matter. Miss D. could not yet have had time to get to know all the servants in the house

by sight. Servants in Scotland are very ten-
acious of their supposed right to attend the
funerals of their friends, and never scruple to
take a holiday for that purpose. From which it
results that I have not the slightest doubt that
the figure seen by Johnina was no ghost, but
simply that of some servant on his way to attend
a funeral. But for Miss Euphame, it would
never for a moment have been considered to be
anything else. But it so happens that we have
staying in the house where the figure is seen an
old lady, whose mind is an acknowledged
museum of superstitious notions. Seen through
the magnifying and distorting medium of this
mind, an incident which in reality is a very
simple one, assumes a different complexion.
And, as one fool is known to make many, so no
doubt the fool of this party inoculates every one
of her fellows with some touch of her crazy infatuation. By a *coincidence* so remarkable as
almost to challenge belief, a violent and sudden
death does occur at precisely the time when the
old lady has predicted it—though it is not, as you
will observe, the death of the person on whose
behalf her fears had been aroused. The minds
of the onlookers are excited by the calamity,
and they at once connect two occurrences which
are in reality wholly distinct, attributing to them
the relation of cause and effect. By which simple
means you have your ghost-story."

"But the phenomenon of the voice heard in prayer by Dalziel—your theory does not account for that?"

"That voice, as I have no kind of doubt, was Miss Euphame's. In all probability she occupied the next bedroom to the lawyer's, and in expectation of her approaching dissolution, whilst he lay in slumber, was engaged in devout prayer. It is true that the walls here are too thick to permit such sounds to pass through them; but you will remember that Dalziel states particularly that he had left his window open. As the weather was so hot, Miss Euphame had no doubt done likewise—with the result that the sound was so transmitted. Dalziel, I believe, was fond of giving it as his belief that he had heard the voice at the precise moment when poor Johnina had been engaged in her death-struggle. But he had no possible means of proving that; and I am, therefore, inclined to regard it as his one artistic addition to what is otherwise a plain narrative of facts. Now, S., I hope that you are satisfied?"

"With your story, yes; with your explanation, no."

## AN EXODUS FROM RAT HALL.

"RATS leaving their usual haunts in your houses, barns, and stackyards, and going to the fields, is an unfortunate omen for the person whose abode they leave." So wrote one Wilkie of Bowden, the author of a manuscript collection of old Border customs and superstitions, compiled in the commencement of the present century for the use of Sir Walter Scott. The following incident illustrating the belief is related as having occurred upon the estate of the present writer. In the early years of the present century, the farm of Maisondieu was tenanted by a family named Fortune, who had been for several generations in occupation, and were reputed to have held land in the neighbourhood for above two hundred years. The name Maisondieu, it may be stated in passing, was derived from a religious house, or hospital, "for the reception of pilgrims, the diseased, and the indigent," which had formerly stood upon the present farm lands.

At last a crisis in the history of the Fortune family arrived. The old farmer died, leaving a

son of some three or four and twenty years of
age to succeed him. Robert Fortune, the
younger, was a fine young man, who lacked not
spirit or ability so much as principle and steadiness. Left to his own devices, with money in
his pocket, and without guide, monitor, or con-
troller, he seemed to have set himself to dissipate
alike the reputation and the fortune which had
been acquired through the prudence and good
conduct of his forebears. He had enrolled
himself a member of a local corps of Yeomanry
Cavalry, which had been raised in the expectation of a French Invasion; and he was bent
upon cutting a dash. He prided himself upon
the horses he rode; and many were the scenes
of midnight carousal, and of hare-brained
prank and horse-play, enacted by himself and
his hot-blooded, would-be fire-eating companions
in the old farm-house at this period. For a brief
time things went as merrily as the marriage
bell of the proverb; but then a change set in.
Peace was proclaimed, and farmers' prices, which
the war had kept high, fell. A succession of
bad seasons followed; and, instead of meeting
them by retrenchment, young Fortune turned
for consolation in the troubles which they
brought him to a still more reckless extrava-
gance. His elders shook their heads, and
people began to say, when his back was turned,
that he was going to the dogs. In time, the

pinch of poverty began to be felt at Maisondieu. The Yeomanry had been disbanded, and Robert now sat alone by his black hearth. To drive out the cold, and raise his spirits to the pitch which they had known in happy bygone days, he resorted to the bottle. This, of course, made matters worse. He neglected his business, his accounts were not kept, and his affairs became disordered. The house fell into a state of disrepair, which, being allowed to continue, grew rapidly worse; and the servants, observing their master's weakness, ceased to respect him, and at last, being gained upon by a feeling that he was a man who was going fast down the hill, took to scamping their work or shirking it.

But, if he found himself deserted by his boon companions—friends of a summer day—a new set of associates began to gather in force about poor Bob. If, instead of describing him as going "to the dogs," people had said to the "rats," it would have been more literally correct. Only it was the rats who came to him. They had long infested the farmyard, and now, in the general relaxing of former strictness, they had succeeded in effecting an entrance into the house. And having once entered, they held the advantage they had gained. At first their presence was only made known at night, after the lights had been put out, and the inmates of the house had withdrawn to bed.

Then, indeed, they held high revels in the kitchen
—as a continual sound of skurrying feet, the
occasional whisking of a tail upon the wainscot,
the overturning with a clatter or a crash of some
vessel of tin or earthenware, or the bold bounding
of some more than commonly intrepid adventurer,
allowed all men to be aware. So long they were
heard, and their devastations were felt; but the
devastators were not seen. But, in course of
time, finding themselves masters of the situation,
they grew bolder, and ventured abroad by daylight too. Then it came to be no uncommon
sight to see a rat cross the passage in front of
you ; or, on entering the kitchen, to catch sight of
one suspended by his fore-feet, his tail depend-
ing behind him, sampling the contents of some
butter-jar, or dripping-pot, which had been left
unlidded on the table. When he saw himself
detected, the rat would beat a leisurely retreat,
and there was insolence in his carriage and in
the sweep of his tail, as though he knew his
adversary's weakness. It was observed at this
time that though the farmer, his man, and maid,
grew lean, the rats on the farm grew fat. At last,
with high living and impunity, their boldness
grew beyond all bounds, and from the kitchen
they extended their playground so as to comprise
the whole house. Then it became a common
occurrence for a rat to run across you whilst you
lay in bed ; or, if your toes peeped out at the

"THE SHEPHERD WATCHED THE SPECTACLE."

*New Border Tales.*]

foot of a short coverlet, for you to feel one nibbling at them. Or a rat might even hang feeding on the draught-blown, guttering candle at the farmer's very elbow, whilst he himself sat late into the night, plunged in a heavy reverie, the result, in equal parts, of his troubles and his potations. So is it with a certain class of humanity, who feed and flourish amid the misfortune and the decline of their betters. The depredations committed were enormous ; for when they could not spoil or devour food or other property, the rats would carry it away. No contrivance was of the smallest use against them, for they soon understood the nature of the most ingenious trap, whilst poison failed to tempt them. Thus, whilst increasing in size, they increased so amazingly in numbers that—its owner being by this time so down in the world as to appear a safe butt for insolence—the old and formerly much respected house of Maisondieu now received from the profane the nickname of " Rat Hall."

It was about this time that the remarkable incident with which my story is concerned was witnessed by an old shepherd in Fortune's service. The family of Hall, a race of shepherds, had been long associated with that of Fortune upon the farm of Maisondieu, and old Bauldy, its present representative, was now, in its own phrase, " the fourth generation serving the fourth generation." Greatly older and by nature more thoughtful than his master, he, of course, viewed the state of matters on the farm with a heavy heart, and looked forward with the gloomiest forebodings to the time when, as it seemed, he must inevitably be separated from that master, whom, in spite of faults, he loved, and from the spot where he had spent a long and happy life-time. Well, one night in spring-time, he was sadly returning to the onstead after a visit to his lambs. A brilliant moon rode in a clear sky, and as he skirted an old hedge which separates the farm premises from a field, at that time in grass, he saw before him a single rat.

"Bad luck to you!" he murmured, under his breath, "for ye have brought bad luck on us."

The rat, which had come out of a rat-hole in the bank (which was perfectly riddled with them), now seemed to look about him. The shepherd watched it. Returning to the hole, it re-appeared, accompanied by a second rat. They in turn looked about them, and perhaps compared notes as to what they saw, for this time one only retired to the hole. It was absent during some moments, and then returned, bringing with it a very large old rat, which it piloted with care. The hair upon the face of the old rat was white with age; and the shepherd observed that it was blind. His interest was by this time thoroughly aroused, and grasping his tall crook with both hands, he rested his cheek against his arms and watched, intently and in silence, from the black shadow of the hedge. And now he witnessed what amazed him. From each of the innumerable rat-holes in the hedge-row, as if by magic, as if from a child's toy, there had started forth a rat, which now crouched, motionless and listening, before the entrance to its cave. Their number, and the uniformity of their action, gave to the effect presented the dignity of impressiveness. It was quite clear that they were acting, not by chance, but in the prosecution of some well-thought-out plan, upon some preconcerted signal. As he watched them, Old Bauldy scarce drew his breath. The night was still; and when they had apparently satisfied themselves that the coast was clear, the rats advanced a little way. And as, in doing so, they brought their tails and hind-quarters clear of the mouths of the rat-holes, they disclosed the nozzles and bright bead-like eyes of other rats behind them. If it had been curiosity which had at first kept the shepherd motionless, it was the instinct of self-preservation which did so now. An army of rats such as he now beheld might well inspire uneasiness, nay, terror, in a braver man ; and, as he gazed, its numbers were being every moment reinforced. For now, above the living silence of a country landscape contemplated by night, a

low, but ever gathering and growing rumour was
gradually making itself heard.  It came from
underground, and it was produced by the beating of many thousands of little feet upon the
trodden earth of the runs.  And, at last, whilst
the sound increased in volume, by a hundred
mouths the earth began to disgorge its living
burthen.  Rats!  They were of the Norway
breed, and first in order came the great males.
These are used to live alone; if hunger presses
them they will prey upon their own brood; they
justly inspire terror.  The less formidable females
followed, each accompanied by her young.
And ever as they swarmed in momentarily
increasing numbers, as in the remote historical
or mythical Migration of the Nations, the rear
rank pushed the front rank before it, till the rats
spread far afield, and the very ground seemed
alive and moving with their multitudes.  Trans-
fixed in the attitude which he had at first
assumed, the shepherd watched the spectacle—
standing like a man who has been turned to
stone, whom no earthly power could have in-
duced to stir a finger.  To say that never in his
life before had he seen so many rats would be to
utter idlest words.  In no agonised vision of the
night, lying stretched upon his pallet of "cauf,"
whilst his breath froze, and his enemies disported
themselves triumphantly, insultingly, upon the
bare boards of the loft, peeped in on by a

mischievous moon, had he ever *dreamed* of so many!

As has been said, during all this time it had been amply apparent that the rats were not acting without some plan of their own.  Instead of following each one his own bent, they moved with the regularity and the discipline of trained forces manœuvring in order.  Nothing could have less resembled the blind infatuation of their fellows and predecessors, who had frisked at the heels of the Pied Piper through the streets of Hamelin to their doom.  They had far more in common with the grim determination of the instruments of vengeance against Bishop Hatto.  But their demeanour, if a little stern, was calm as well as resolute, as, inspired by a single purpose, controlled by a single will, they advanced, marching shoulder to shoulder.  There were few stragglers, few weak places in their ranks.  Their *morale* was very nearly perfect.

And now, when they had wheeled into the field, a touching incident occurred.  The old hoary-faced rat had undoubtedly in his youth been marked by nature for a leader.  But times were changed; he was old and blind, and for a moment he stood helpless before his people.  For a moment, but no longer.  Grasping the position of affairs, the rat who had been the first to appear, stepped forward to the rescue,

and saved the situation. In his mouth he was
observed to hold, by one of its ends, a straw—
the other end of which he now dextrously
inserted betwixt the jaws of the Patriarch, so as
to form a sort of leading-string. And, thus
coupled, the two rats moved off, and were
followed by their thousands,—the old rat,
through the graceful intervention of the young
one, still preserving every tittle of his dignity as
a king and father of his people, into whose
mouth, in this momentous crisis of his reign, the
poet might well have put the words:

> "Quo nos cunque feret melior fortuna parente
> Ibimus, o socii!"

The shepherd watched the moving mass, as it
passed across the moonlit surface of the field,
like the shadow of a cloud, until at last it was
lost to sight beyond a rising ground.

Then, and not till then, did he stir. Pulling
himself hastily together, he made for the farm-
house, and with the freedom allowed to an old
servant, burst into his master's room. Fortune
was seated at the table, his face buried in his
hands. A sheet of printed paper lay before
him.

"Bob! Bob!" cried the old man, "we are
presairved—the rats are gone!"

But Bob only lifted a heavy head and pointed
without speaking to the paper which lay before

him.   It was an announcement that a "dis-
plenishing sale" would shortly be held at
Maisondieu.

"Lord! and has it come to this?"

"It has, indeed!   I had not the heart to
break it to you before, Bauldy."   And then he
added with bitterness, "We must have the
usual jollification, I suppose.   Well, there will
be meat for many to provide that day; but I
doubt 'twill be the poison of one."

And so, sure enough, ere the Whitsuntide
term-day arrived, the furniture and fittings of
Maisondieu farm had fallen to the auctioneer's
hammer; and Robert Fortune and his old and
faithful shepherd had gone forth homeless, and
in opposite directions, to face and fight the
world.

It only remains to add that this story, wild as
it may appear, is, in its main facts, currently
related at the present day among the country-
people of Roxburghshire.

# THE BRITHER STANES.

## I.

STORIES of fraternal enmity are not uncommon throughout the country. In the Lammermuir hills, the Twinlaw Cairns are said to commemorate two brothers, who meeting by chance, after long separation, in the opposing ranks of a battle, fell by each other's hands. Again, the farmhouse of Hallow Down, situated to the northwest of the only seaport of the Merse, is the reputed scene of a wild tale of smuggling adventure and of brotherly treachery which has been made the subject of a play. At the root of such popular stories and traditions there often lies a human truth of the deepest and best ascertained kind. In the physical world extremes meet; does this axiom also hold good in the world of mind and feeling; and is it true that the extreme of nearness may, with perilous ease, become the extreme of opposition? Upon the rough ridge of a moor or hill, in the parish of Mertoun, are to be seen, confronting each other a short way apart, two upright blocks of whinstone. They

are known to the country people as the Brothers'
Stones, and they also commemorate a tragedy.

Ninian Cranstoun, of Third, a small landowner,
representing a younger branch of a local family
which had once been powerful, was in his day
notorious for his overbearing temper and high-
handed ways.   His disposition tended to the
roistering and convivial; but so ungovernable
were his passions, especially when inflamed by
drink, so impatient was he of the smallest cross,
that, whilst still in the prime of a vigorous manhood, he had already quarrelled beyond hope of
a reconciliation with almost every one of his
friends and neighbours.   The isolated life which
resulted from these alienations did not agree
with him, and his exacerbated temper wreaked
itself upon his dependents and inferiors, whom
he bullied and domineered over daily more and
more.   At last one night, when he had been
attending St. Boswells' Fair, he failed to return
home; and next morning his body was discovered by the wayside, where it had manifestly
been made the subject of a brutal murder.
Little of surprise and less of regret were felt in
the popular mind when the news became known;
and, in further proof of the degree in which the
murdered man had been hated and detested, it
may be stated that the perpetrators of the out-
rage were never discovered.   There were marks
upon the road of a prolonged and violent

4

struggle; and the spot where the crime was committed was close to a corner of the fair ground, where the cries of the victim for help must have been heard. This corner of the Green was, however, that occupied by the gipsies, who attended the fair in large numbers. Laird Cranstoun was known to have incurred the wrath of these vagrants, and suspicion at once attached itself to them. But though a reward for the detection of the criminal was offered, and though there were probably several hands concerned in the crime, and no less probably many accessories after the fact, a tacit freemasonry seemed to shield the murderers from discovery, and (as has been already said) they were never brought to justice.

All this, however, is incidental. What concerns us here is a scene which was enacted at the Third when the murdered man's body was brought home. The corpse had been placed on a rude, improvised bier; and, covered with a sheet, was borne along homeward by four labouring men. As they passed by, the rumour of the deed of violence (which had preceded them) attracted the gossips to the wayside; where, seeing that the bier was already followed by idlers from the fair, many of them also were impelled to join the procession. For this purpose, as if attracted by a fascination which they could not resist, hinds and bondagers left their labours in the fields, and women, who had come with their children to the cottage door, their dwellings. So, as it proceeded, the procession swelled and grew. No person seemed to regard distance. And the feature which gave its special character to the crowd was its essential unconcern. There was plenty of interest manifested, plenty of gluttonous curiosity; but of horror, or of sorrow, so far, none.

At last the transit was accomplished, and the bearers set down their burthen in the vestibule of the house of Third. A few of the followers had ere this dropped off; but many persevered. These now availed themselves of the confusion to push through the unclosed door and edge their way into the house. The deceased man's widow was coming down the stairs, and when her eye fell upon the sheet (which was blood-stained), and upon the partially defined outline of that which it covered, she shrieked aloud. Then, all at once, the women raised a sympathetic cry—

"Och, how! Och, how! 'tis cruel wark."

But, at that very moment, a cry of a different and more alarming character diverted their attention. It proceeded from an adjoining room. One of the bystanders, a woman who was standing nearest, hurriedly went out and returned bearing in her arms a boy of eight or nine years. The child's face was suffused with

blood which flowed from a wound near the left
temple. Instantly the corpse was forgotten,
and attention centred on this new disaster.
The boy was Walter, the younger of the twin
sons left behind by Ninian Cranstoun; and it
was discovered that the wound on his forehead
had been received whilst he was wrangling with
his brother. Upon examination it promised to
be nothing worse than a severe cut, which would
probably leave a permanent scar; but all the
volunteering nurses and advisers were agreed
that, had its position varied by half an inch or
so, it would certainly have been fatal. After
consternation and sympathy on the part of the
gossips, came indignation. The foolish, emotional women had already had their feelings
worked upon, and as soon as the injured child
had begun to receive attention, those of them
who were not otherwise employed turned upon
the elder boy, who had been instrumental in inflicting the injury. He stood by with a callous air.

"He cannot let his brother be!" exclaimed
one of the women, who was a neighbour; "day
and night he's forever tormenting him."

"He'll be the death of the poor callant one o'
these days," returned a second.

"Sure the devil's in ye, boy."

Many more such speeches were delivered.
Meanwhile the object against whom they were
directed struggled manfully to preserve a pro-

vokingly unconcerned demeanour. But that
this was not a true index to the state of his
mind was apparent from the way in which the
veins in his forehead had grown dark and stood
out, and from the nervous persistency with
which he nicked with a knife at a stick which he
held in his hand and was whittling. Perhaps
he felt the injustice of the obloquy directed
against him; for, though it was true that he had
been engaged in a struggle with his brother at
the time when the injury was inflicted, still it
was no less true that the nature and extent
of that injury were entirely the result of accident.
As the two boys wrestled together, they had
fallen to the ground, and the head of the
younger, as he fell, had come in violent contact
with the sharp corner of a piece of furniture,
which had done the mischief. But women,
when their feelings are aroused by the sight of
supposed barbarity, are not inclined to inquire
into the facts of a case; and young Ninian, who
had inherited his father's temper, as well as his
name, would have died sooner than condescend
to open his lips in self-justification.

As the women continued to relieve their
feelings at the boy's expense, there was one
speech of sinister foreboding uttered which,
being heard by many, was in after days recalled.
The speaker was a certain elderly woman named
Magdalen, or more familiarly Mause, whose

height of stature and strength of character had combined to give her some authority in the neighbourhood.   On the other hand, partly because she pretended to knowledge which other people had not, partly because her dwelling stood apart from others, she had in some quarters come to be looked upon as a witch, and suspected of holding communication with the Evil One.   This was a character which she did not seek to repudiate.

"There will be mair bluid spilt, mair life ta'en, yet," quoth this gaunt, grey-haired sibyl, when she had glanced significantly on the bier. "'Twas fated sae to be, and ilk ane maun dree his weird."

There was not a bystander present but at once understood her allusion.  Her words had reference to a saying to which no other person present would have had the hardihood to allude; and in being the one to do so, Mause was consistent to her system of showing herself superior to vulgar prejudice.   In those days a sufficient belief still clung about the popular sayings or "prophecies," which are commonly (though no doubt mistakenly) attributed to Thomas the Rhymer, to bring it about that such of them as are of ill omen should by general consent be tabooed.   Now there is one of these sayings which declares that *Cranstoun's hand is against Cranstoun.*

By this time the forehead of the wounded boy
had been bathed and dressed ; and, soothed upon
his mother's knee, his plaint was stilled.    The
on-lookers felt that they had now no longer any
pretext for remaining, and lingeringly, and with
many a last word, they withdrew and dispersed
in the directions of their homes.

II.

AFTER her husband's death, Mrs. Cranstoun
continued to live on at the Third, and to bring
up her sons.    Her task was not an easy one.
Each of the boys had inherited a considerable
share of his father's disposition, Walter resembling him most in his high spirits and love
of wild pranks, Ninian in the morose and sullen
moods to which the elder Cranstoun had in his
later years been subject.    Mrs. Cranstoun loved
her sons equally ; but it is needless to say which
of the two boys was the favourite with the rest
of the world.    In addition to possessing superior
social qualities, though the two young men were
much alike, Walter was rather better-looking
than his brother, and had also slightly the advantage of him in stature.    Hence there arose
between them that particular kind of rivalry, not
to say jealousy, which is met with when, of two
brothers, one is the favourite and the other is
the heir.    As boys they had at times shown
signs of cherishing the peculiar fervour of mutual

attachment and of experiencing the singular intensity of mutual sympathy which are peculiar
to twins. But even as boys they had exchanged
many more blows than caresses. Walter still
bore on his left eyebrow a small white angular
scar, over which the hair did not grow, to keep
him in mind of the injury which he had received
when a child. And, as the lads grew up, their
mother saw with grief and with a sense of foreboding, that an estrangement was springing up
between them. They still shared each other's pas-
times, but the superior skill of Walter in all manly
sports was a source of constant annoyance to his
brother. And to make matters worse, Walter was
a boy who took a mischievous pleasure in tormenting others, whilst Ninian's was a disposition in
which a slight, or injury, rankled—so that often,
after receiving some perhaps merely fancied
ground of offence, he would allow days to pass
before he would again speak to his brother.

At last, one fine spring morning, Walter,
sauntering aimlessly about the precincts of the
farm, encountered Ninian and accosted him.
There had recently been a disagreement between
them, and they had not spoken to each other for
some days. Whether it was in the spirit of
provocation or of conciliation that Walter now
spoke is not clear. But if his intentions
were friendly, his choice of an overture was,
to say the least of it, ill-advised ; for, though

he well knew (had he troubled to reflect) both his brother's dislike to being beaten and his own superiority in the game, he now proposed a match at stone-chucking. Ninian, who had a book in his hand, declined the challenge civilly enough; whereupon Walter proposed a trial of skill at quoits instead. But Nean (as he was always called for short) did not wish to play at quoits either. However, Walter was not to be said nay. His temper disposed him to mischief, and he continued to importune his elder brother, hoping, either by coaxing or by taunts, to tease him into compliance with his wishes. Nean was by no means one who could stand much teasing; however, this morning he kept his temper better than usual, and at last, when he saw that Walter was not to be beaten off, agreed to meet him in a match, not of stone-chucking or of quoiting, but of wrestling. This choice was again an unlucky one; for, whatever may be said to the contrary, it is never an easy task to maintain perfect coolness and composure in a keenly contested match either of boxing or of wrestling.

> "Juego de manos,
>    Juego de villanos,"

says an old Spanish proverb.

The match being agreed upon, the two youths straightway walked off in silence, side by side, through the beauty of the May morning. They came to a green field, lying near the house and below it. This field is bounded by a little babbling brook, which has a singularly zig-zag course. The ground on the banks is uneven; and the brook is shaded by a grove of old trees, of which one or two are broken, whilst others have had their roots laid bare by the action of the water. This was the scene of many a boyish contest; and here, selecting level ground, with one consent, they paused. Nean then divested himself of his tunic and belt; but it so happened that Walter, who had assumed a slight air of bravado, kept his belt on. In this belt—in accordance with a fashion which was common among spirited young men of that day—he carried, in its sheath, a little dirk. The brothers then confronted each other. They were two fine muscular young men, and in a wrestling bout were less unequally mated than elsewhere; since if Walter had the activity and the science, the advantage in weight and strength was on the side of his brother.

Falling vigorously to the play, Ninian at once grasped his adversary low down upon the waist; but Walter, feeling that he was had at a disadvantage, wisely delayed taking hold. In this manner some minutes had been spent in ineffectual fumbling, and Nean, whose patience was beginning to be taxed, had insensibly allowed his grasp to slip somewhat higher up his brother's back, when with a sudden hitch—a ram-like movement—Walter grappled with him. They were now "in grips." But Nean's arms, deprived suddenly of their support, had slipped close to his brother's neck. Swift as thought, Walter seized his opportunity, wheeled, and executing an almost complete revolution, employed the throw which is known as the "buttock,"—lifting his brother clean off the ground, and throwing him head over heels. Nean fell heavily on his shoulder, and arose considerably shaken.

The brothers faced each other again, and this time Walter, reversing his former tactics, grappled immediately, and almost as soon threw his antagonist—drawing him on to his knee by means of what is called in the game a "snap,"— a trick which is accounted somewhat dubious wrestling.

Once more the two young men confronted each other, panting. His heavy fall, followed by this questionable piece of play, had roused the less vivacious elder brother, and put him on his mettle. He seemed determined not to be flung again, and the third bout was by far the longest of the three. In vain did Walter essay the "hipe," the "inside cleik," the "outside stroke"; his brother, now upon the defensive, was wary and stood his ground. At last, when it seemed that Walter must be about wearied out, Nean prepared to try the throw which his superior power and

weight had made his favourite and most successful one. Putting forth his strength, and lifting
his younger brother fairly off the ground, he
swung him round in his arms like a child. But
Walter's science was too much for him. Keeping
his feet, whilst in the air, extended as far as they
would go, he avoided being tripped upon being
set down; whilst no sooner had he touched the
ground than he quickly had recourse to the
"back heel," — throwing his brother heavily
on his back, and himself falling on the top of him.

But the cry which burst from Ninian's lips, as
he touched earth, was not that of a mere defeated
athlete. Bounding to his feet, Walter saw at
a glance what had happened. In his whirling
flight through space, the little dirk which he wore
at his thigh had escaped from its sheath, and
when the wrestlers fell together its blade had
been pressed against the side of the undermost
of them, inflicting a wound from which the blood
was now flowing freely. Ninian lay back upon
the grass, and uttered no reproach.

Overcome with horror, Walter cast about for
some means of succouring the wounded lad. To
run back to the house would take too long, so
tearing a strip from his own shirt, he knelt down,
and supporting his brother's head, endeavoured
to bind up the wound. But his unskilful efforts
were of no avail. The blood flowed on; the
bandage was saturated.

Ninian spoke.

" Try to stanch the blood."

Then Walter tore off another strip of shirt, crumpled it up, and pressed it firmly to the wound. But, after a moment, the dark fluid stained it.

Nean lay back motionless ; but the love of life still fought in him.

"Watty, take my hat, and fetch water from the burn, and bathe the wound."

In an agony of haste, Watty flew to obey. He bathed the wound; but the blood flowed ever.

" It is of no use."

There was silence. Ninian lay back, patient with the pathetic patience of growing weakness. Watty, seated behind him on the grass, tenderly supported the sinking form against his shoulder. The sun shone, the breezes blew, the water flowed. A bird spoke sweetly from a tree.

" Water."

That thirst which follows hemorrhage, and is ofttimes the precursor of death, had invaded the sinking man. Gently Walter laid him down, fetched water, and set it to his lips. Even as he did so, a film seemed to pass over his brother's eye, and he felt that this was death. He could support no more. Stooping, he pressed his lips with an agonised fervour to his brother's, a single sob convulsed his frame, and he fled across the fields towards home.

His mother was seated in the parlour. From her window she had that morning beheld her sons go forth in amity, for the first time for many a day; and she now nursed pleasing delusions, the offspring of the sight.

"Is that you, Walter?" said she, as the boy came in, "I am glad to see you. Where is your brother?"

"Am I his keeper?"

The words and the tone of the reply startled her.

"Why, no!" she answered, commanding herself so as to smile, "certainly you are not his keeper, but I saw you go out together an hour agone."

"Well, mother, Nean is in the cow pasture, and he wishes you to go to him."

"I will. What is he doing?"

Walter paused for a moment before replying. Then he said:

"Mother! by now, he is asleep."

Filled with a vague sense that the hour she had lived in dread of had come at last, Mrs. Cranstoun hurriedly left the house. And as she left it by one door, Wat left it by another.

### III.

As the result of the accident in the wrestling-match, Mrs. Cranstoun lost one of her sons; but not the elder. Ninian's wound was not mortal, and after hovering between life and death, his mother's care at length restored him to health. But from the time of her brief interview with her second son, after the accident, Mrs. Cranstoun saw Walter no more. Firmly believing that his brother, if not already dead, lay at the point of death, on leaving the house he had fled from the neighbourhood. An agony of remorse for his unintentional act drove him forth. Perhaps, also, his feelings were complicated by a dread of being suspected of having murdered his brother. Appearances were against him; his temper was known to be violent, and the relations which had subsisted between the two lads were known to be strained. In any case, he was seen no more at Third, nor were tidings of him received there. Even before the occurrence of the unfortunate incident which had driven him to flight, he had shown signs that he was growing tired of home, and it remained to be surmised that that incident had been the means of suddenly developing a roving disposition in him.

Years passed. Mrs. Cranstoun died, and her elder son lived on upon his patrimony. And his onward course in time was a downward course in character. In the conditions of his life there were met three factors, regarding the concurrence of which the present writer, when in the course of these tales he shall come to tell the story of the Seamy Side of Country Life, will have enough to say. In the meantime suffice it to state that these three factors are : solitude; lack of occupation; and a competency. Taken together they have proved too much for many a better man than Cranstoun. As he had grown older and become his own master, the moroseness and violence of his temper had increased. He had shunned the salutary correcting influences which act upon the man who leads his life as one in a community, and his faults had become confirmed. Time and favouring circumstance had brought out the hereditary faults in his character, which showed themselves now, not only in violence, but in intemperance and the passion of the gamester.

Some thirty years had passed since the scene in the cow-pasture, when, one afternoon, the laird of Third was returning home from a distant village whither some transaction of farmer's business had called him. He was on horseback. The season was autumn, and the day was dull, with gusts of wind and passing showers. But the heaven of the rider's mind was yet more sombre and clouded than the sky. He was suffering from the painful depression, complicated with irritability of the nerves, which often follows excessive drinking.

In the course of his homeward way he had to pass over a wide open green or common. It was the spot where, many years before, his father had been murdered. Here, in one of the angles formed by a cross-road, opposite a finger-post, there was a little inn, or change-house. Cranstoun had been looking forward to the refreshment which was to be obtained there, and when he got to the door he shouted. But the old man who kept the place had been called away on some business of his own, and there was no reply. However, the thirsty customer was not baffled. He alighted, tethered his mare to the post, and then, finding that the inn-door was locked, broke a pane of glass, pushed back the window-bolt, and entered by one of the windows.

As a patron of the house, he knew where the landlord kept his liquor, as well as where the key of the receptacle was hidden when he was away. So he was soon seated at a table with a bottle and glass before him. The drink—Hollands, landed duty-free at Eyemouth—was sound and potent ; and as Cranstoun sat on over it, the dim light of the autumn afternoon faded imperceptibly from the sky. His attitude was that of a man thinking deeply. Meanwhile his beast, exposed to spirts of rain and to the blasts of a wind which toward nightfall had grown blustering, grew fidgety and champed her bit.

The roads leading north, south, east, and west were little travelled that day. At last, however, the toper was startled from his reveries by a double knock at the door.

"What ho! within."

His first impulse had been to disregard the summons ; then he thought differently. When he had drawn the bolt, he found himself face to face with a tall and powerfully built stranger in a flowing cloak, who, mistaking him for the land-lord, swore at him for keeping the door locked. Cranstoun, who was taciturn, did not explain the mistake. The stranger appeared to be some swaggerer who affected an extravagant style in his discourse.

"Mine host of the Garter!" was his exclama-tion, on gaining admittance. "Ha! and, for lack of custom, engaged in proving his own vintages. This is of good omen—take a traveller's word for it! My friend, I am not yet at my journey's end, but I'll bear ye company a while."

Still without speaking, Cranstoun pushed a drinking-horn towards him, which the new-comer filled from the bottle, drained and filled again.

> "The road is lanesome, dark the night,
>     And cauld the welcome there, my jo!"

sang he ; "but 'tis the liquor, the liquor, that's the thing."

And then, breaking off to complain of the darkness, the intruder called for a light. Crans-

toun, who for some reason chose to fall in with
his humour, set the wick of a candle to the
"gathering coal" in the grate, and placed it on
the table. Then he made out—what he had not
noticed before—that the chance comer wore a
soldier's uniform. And to judge from its patched
and tattered condition, as well as from the wearer's
seamed and sunburnt aspect, he appeared to
have seen much military service. Probably he
was one of those soldiers of fortune, of whom
Dalgetty is the type, who, two hundred years
ago, made war their trade—the element in which
they lived. And perhaps he was now returning
to his home ; but if any "Cousin Jean" chanced
to await him there, that lady could never be
blamed did she obey her instinct and shut the
house-door in the face of a "stoure carle" so
questionable of aspect. But Ninian suffered no
recoil from the stranger ; indeed, he had no right
to do so, for the twin silhouettes now thrown by
the candle-flame upon the wall resembled each
other strikingly.

"Well !" quoth the soldier, as he set his cup
down, "time is time, and I must be travelling.
How dark it is grown ! but 'twould take a darker
night than this to make me miss the way. Why,
brother, I were born an' bred i' these parts—tho'
there was no inn here, I think, in those days.
It is a wish to visit the old scenes again which
now brings me back."

"You have kin hereabouts, no doubt ? " asked Ninian.

"No, no. They're dead—they must be dead," returned the other softly.

The reckoning now falling to be paid, the soldier drew out a coin to discharge it with; but, on a second thought, proposed a hazard. Cranstoun assented, the coin spun, and the soldier won the toss; as he did again when they tossed for double or quits. The loser cursed his luck and laughed.

" I know a game worth two of that," remarked the unknown, "if I'd only time to stop and play it."

" What is your game? "

Without speaking, the wanderer drew a chestnut from his pouch, removed the shell, and with the aid of a knife began to fashion from the kernel a small neat cube. Seeming by intuition to divine his intention, the other meantime charred a stick, which he had previously pointed, in the candle-flame. The cube, when duly branded with the stick, formed a rude die. Using one of the two horn tumblers as a dice-box, the men tested it. It was true.

" Just one main," said Ninian. Thereupon they took seats facing each other at the table, and the game began. It soon became plain that each of the players possessed the true gambler's spirit. The game progressed with varying fortune, but on the whole the soldier won. When the two men had sat down (had it been known), he had had but one guinea in his possession; whilst Cranstoun had with him a bag containing thirty guineas—the price of some cattle he had just sold. But, at the end of an hour's play, the financial positions of the players had been precisely reversed. Then Ninian staked his last guinea and lost. Then he staked the saddle and bridle on the horse which stood at the door; and, losing again, risked the animal herself.

" This must be my last stake."

" Why so? You've other property in the house."

" Damn you—I am not the owner of the house."

" Who the devil are you then ? "

" A customer like yourself."

This time Ninian won the throw, and luck's turning-point seemed to have been reached, for he now won back his saddle, won back his bridle, and began to win back his guineas. As the gamblers played, they found frequent excuses for drinking,—the winner toasting his success, the loser resorting to artificial means to keep him from losing heart as well as money. And, as one of the horns was in use as a dice-box, they drank from the same cup. It was not the first time in their lives that they had done so.

Now, except for such as have been schooled in polished society, to gamble heavily without loss of temper is almost as difficult a thing as to wrestle or to box; and more than one hazardous remark had already passed between the players. Chance was now consistently favouring Ninian; and at last, finding that he had won back half the sum which he had originally lost, and wishing to end the game, he proposed to stake this sum upon a single cast of the die against what remained of the soldier's winnings.

" Done with you."

Ninian was the first to throw. He threw a five.

" One chance remains," exclaimed the soldier, fingering the die, "and one only. Now, Goddess Fortune, befriend your votary ! "

In the desire to appear calm, he had resumed his mock-heroic tones; yet, as he spoke, he trembled. Ninian, confident that the game was his, looked on without caring. The die rattled in the box, fell, and sure enough, as if the soldier's prayer had been heard, it turned up six.

" Fortune's a woman after all," said the winner blandly, "and woman is the soldier's friend as well as his divinity. Hand over the stakes."

But he had exulted too soon. His rival had already snatched up the die, and was scrutinising it. His suspicions proved well grounded. Into the yielding substance of which it was composed, exactly upon the brand which marked the ace, had been pressed a pellet of sparrow shot. Its weight had sufficed to turn the scale, and, as Ninian now saw, the soldier had won the last throw by foul means.

"Scoundrel!"

The dishonest player was knocked backward in his seat, his head struck the wall, hands grasped his throat. Then the two men glared at each other face to face, and as they did so the filmy, fluctuating veil which had hung between them melted. It was too late. All the evil passions in the brothers' breasts were roused. Pinned to the wall, the soldier gasped and choked. His eyes were starting from his head. Then, with a sudden active movement—an expiring effort—he started aside and was free. The jerk threw Ninian forward, and his face struck the wall. The horn-handled knife which had been used during the evening, lay on the table. The stranger swept it into his hand. There was a swift movement, a grating sound, a maddened cry; and, like a man bitten by a reptile, Cranstoun bounded to his feet and fled for his life round the narrow room. Catching up a three-legged stool with which to finish him, and raising it over his head, the soldier pursued. But at that moment an unexpected diversion was created. A weird sound, between a sigh and a gasp, which proceeded from neither of the men, was heard by both of them.  To the soldier, it seemed to come from behind him, and he turned his head.

The sigh, or suppressed cry, had been uttered by a woman, a homeless and benighted wanderer, who, attracted like a night-bird or a moth to the lighted window-pane, had gazed for an instant on the horrible picture within and then fled away.  But her terror-frozen cry changed the fortune of the day.  Peering over his shoulder as he stumbled forward, Ninian saw his pursuer turn his head.  He recognised his opportunity.  The heavy stone bottle, or greybeard, which had held the drink, remained on the table.  He seized it by the neck, and, using it like a club, dealt a blow with all his force on the back of his pursuer's head.  Without a cry the soldier fell ; nor did he stir again.  Then Cranstoun raised the candle, and gazed in his face.  There were several scars there, and among them was one small white one of angular form, at the eyebrow, over which the hair did not grow.  Cranstoun set down the candle, turned away and left the house.  His horse still stood at the door.  He unfastened the tether, and as he did so he lurched against the finger-post.

" The night air after the liquor ! " were his words.

He mounted.  The horse, which was a young one, chilled by waiting, and impatient for her

stable, fretted and chafed beneath him. The rider
found it necessary to restrain her, for the night
was very dark. But, presently, his eyes seemed
to have grown accustomed to the darkness.
The little mare broke into a trot, and from a
trot into a canter, and from a canter into a
gallop. She knew the way home, and the rider
had given her the rein. But when, next morning, at the Third, she whinnied to the early
labourer, the body of Ninian Cranstoun dragged
behind her from the stirrup. Life was extinct,
and among the many lesser injuries and dis-
figurements which the body bore, there was one
deep-cut knife-wound in the back, which had
clearly been the cause of death. The story of
the murder of the previous laird of Third was
brought to mind, and was at first connected with
this tragedy. But another story soon floated
through the district. It originated with the
female vagrant, but the origin of such stories is
soon lost sight of. The body found in the ale-
house was, however, identified as that of the
long-lost Walter; and the credulous vulgar,
which delights in nothing more than in supping
its fill of horrors, received with avidity the tale
of the internecine battle between the brothers,—
to commemorate which some hand now forgotten raised the stones on the hill above Third.
The spot where they stand to the present day
bears the name of Brotherston.

The Borderers of a few generations back were scarcely less elemental in their passions than were the Greeks out of whose traditions Æschylus made his tragedies. Only they were more moody and fantastic than the Greeks. Reflecting upon the story just told, we may almost enter into the old dark pagan belief in "some god"—a blind force working in circumstance. And so, in life, we may sometimes see, if we look about us, as it were, something *trying to happen*. And at last, sometimes, it does happen.

# JOHN BUNCLE.

BY no means particularly early one fine summer morning, John Buncle, a day-tale labourer of Fogo, in the Merse of Berwickshire, betook himself to his work of breaking stones at the roadside. John had been drinking the night before, and was out of sorts; so that everything seemed to go amiss with him this morning. He set to his work in a feckless, perfunctory manner, not troubling to find the right side of the stones—the way they break most easily; so that, through his own carelessness, his labour was materially augmented. Then, his hammer struck awry, and the flies settled on his face and neck and tickled him; whilst, as the sun rose in the heavens and its rays beat down more directly upon him, he grew ever warmer and warmer until the sweat simply poured from his brow. At last, in a fit of irritation, he flung down his hammer upon the heap of broken road metal, and venting an imprecation, cursed his own lot in particular and that of humanity in general.

"An' when I mind," continued he, "that, but

for ae bite out o' an aple grown in Eden, these
things waud not ha' been—od! but it makes
me mad. Ill-luck to ye, Yeddy, says I! What
took ye to be guided by the weemen-folk,
that ye s'ould pree? Weel may ye now think
shame on yoursel', that hae brought misfortun'
and hardship on thousands o' puir harmless
bodies, like mysel'. Sure ye might ha' known
better; or a better man might hae been set in
your place. Then we s'ould all hae been leading the life o' lairds at this day, and the sweet
o' the brow—my ban upon it!—wad ne'er ha'
been heard o'!"

This soliloquy was spoken aloud, for John
believed that nobody was within earshot. He
was startled, therefore, and a little disconcerted,
when he heard himself accosted in reply. The
voice which addressed him was a mild one, the
words spoken were polite; and, looking round,
he beheld a person who had evidently come
along the road unnoticed whilst his back had
been turned. The stranger was plainly dressed,
in a dark suit; his hair was silvered by age; and
his appearance and expression generally were
venerable and benign. After two or three intro-
ductory remarks, he assumed a firmer tone of
voice, and in a manner which was pitched
exactly midway between jest and earnest, took
the stone-breaker to task, as well upon the
strength of an expression which he had used

as upon the injustice of the impeachment which it had preceded. John—who, to give him his due, was not a bad sort of a fellow—entered readily into the vein and spirit of his chance acquaintance, and endeavoured in his own particular way to turn the laugh against his interlocutor. But, though he had always rather prided himself upon his mastery of the resources of rustic wit and banter, he soon found that, upon this occasion, he had met his match. There was an unexpected vivacity concealed beneath the quiet dignity of the modestly-attired stranger which enabled him to hold his own with ease in the encounter.

There now came into view, round a turning in the road, a handsome coach drawn by a fine pair of horses. It drove up at a leisurely pace, and stopped near the spot where the stranger and Jock were standing. Then a smart footman descended from the box, touched his cockaded hat to the old gentleman (to whose service he evidently belonged), and held the door of the carriage open that he might enter. Upon apprehending that the man to whom he had been talking was the owner of so stylish a turn-out, the master of servants in livery, our Jock all at once grew "shamefast." But, to his surprise, the gentleman pointed to the carriage, and adopting a tone which was at once more friendly and more peremptory than that which

he had used before, invited him to "jump in."
"I shall be glad if you will come home with
me," he added, "to see my house.    And when I
have shown you that, I promise you the very
best dinner you ever had in your life!"

John wondered, but said nothing.    The two
then took their places in the carriage, which
drove off.    After traversing a few miles of
country road, they drove in at the lodge-gates of
a gentleman's park and up an avenue a mile
long, and a hundred yards broad, which was
planted with fine timber trees, and finally
came to a standstill before the door of a
stately mansion, where they alighted.    The
time while dinner was preparing was spent in
viewing the interior of the house, which contained a fine picture-gallery ; and the charming
gardens and pleasure-grounds attached to it.
John saw, and was a good deal impressed ; but
in his modesty he spoke very little.    There were,
of course, many things there which he did not
understand, and his host had the tact not to
weary him with too detailed a survey.    At last
the owner of the house (who had all along
behaved to his guest with a courtesy and a
kindness rather more delicate than what might
be shown to an equal) conducted the stone-
breaker to the dining-room.    Here there was set
forth a repast which was at once appetising to
the palate and delightful to the eye.    In the

*coup d'œil* presented by the table, rich silver
plate took a tone of greyness by contrast with
the surrounding snow-white cloth; whilst the
element of bright and varied colour was supplied by rare hot-house flowers of waxen, or yet
finer, texture. Some lacqueys stood round in
attendance; but these, as their presence would
only have incommoded his guest, their master
with a wave dismissed. He then, in these
words, addressed the bewildered son of toil :—

"My friend, you see before you a table set out
with every delicacy which study, travel, and a
natural aptitude, have in a long lifetime revealed
to a devoted mind. There is everything here, I
might add, which money can buy; but mere
wealth, as *factitious*, I have always on principle
contemned. (To know what you would buy if
you had the money—that is the one thing
needful: that you have it, or not, is of no
moment. But you will not follow me here.)
This repast, John Buncle, I have had prepared
especially with a view to your enjoyment. Eat,
therefore, and welcome, of whatsoever may seem
good to you—with one solitary exception."
Here the speaker paused, and laid his hand
upon a silver dish-cover. "From this dish, and
from this alone," he proceeded, "I desire you to
abstain—understand me, it is *reserved*. Of it, I
forbid you not only to eat, but even to examine
the contents. But I do so with the less reluct-

ance that it contains nothing which could possibly be beneficial to you." So saying, and wishing his guest good appetite, the master of the house withdrew.

Left to himself, our good clown at once regained his ease. He laughed aloud. This, he protested, was the rummest start he had ever met with in his life. He couldn't understand it at all. Then, without more delay, he fell to examining the victuals and tasting of this and that. The dishes contained the appetising, far-fetched, concoctions of a Parisian *cordon bleu*. The flasks were filled with the choicer vintages of France,—in perfume, like to violets or the rose; in colour, amber-clear, or dark with ruby lights; cool to the gullet, sparkling,—liquid inspiration, poetry,—the soul, or finer essence, in a bottle! The weather, as I have mentioned, being warm, some of these drinks were *frappés*.

Our John did not stand upon ceremony. He dipt his fingers where he pleased, spoiled what he chose; and Christopher Sly himself, in the mansion of the rich lord, did not run a more glorious riot. But—alas! for Nature's homely plan—the feast was thrown away upon him,— his rude gullet resembling the trained palate of his patron no more than did his honest horny hand (off which you might have cut corns with a knife) the delicate palm of a lady. However, to do him justice, he did his best to rise to the

"BUT STAY—'TWAS NOT EMPTY."

*New Border Tales.*]

occasion ; and what was wanting in refinement of appreciation was made up for in gross amount.

But whilst he fed (for this is not eating), the "crumpled rose-leaf" was not absent from his couch. In the midst of the fountain of dainties, as the Latin poet sang, there arose a something which vexed him. It was this. From the first, the solitary dish-cover under which he had been forbid to pry had piqued his imagination; and now, in proportion as the appetite of the body became satisfied, the appetite of the mind grew keen. He began to hover round, and to scrutinise the mysterious dish; but he spared to touch it. At last,—when Nature had done her utmost, and could no more,—his curiosity reached a pitch at which it amounted well-nigh to torment. "Why, in the name of justice," he emphatically asked himself, "why, if he were not to do as he pleased, had he been turned loose upon the feast at all?" It was not treating him fairly. He began to smart under a sense of imagined injury, and felt that any gratitude which might be due to his absent host for the food which he had consumed disappeared, entirely disappeared when weighed against his just cause of complaint at having something that he wanted to know kept back from him. And, after all, what had he to be grateful for! There had been nothing here to his fancy. Collops, or a singed sheep's head, or a nice

6

greasy haggis, followed by an appetising
beastin' pudding, such as his wife made when
the cow calved, would in his judgment have
beat all the foreign flummery which had been
set before him.    As for the liquor, the three-
penny ale at The Three Tuns was worth the
whole of it!    And was it not likely that the
forbidden cover interposed betwixt himself and
the very thing (he knew not what that thing was)
which his heart desired?

Impelled by an irresistible fascination, he
again approached the silver lid, and pored
intently upon it.    But it kept its secrets well.
No savoury steaming odour came from beneath
it, to guide the fancy in picturing the hopeless
delicacies which it concealed.    Jock bent nearer,
and sniffed again.    No smell came from the
dish at all; but hark! most unexpectedly, in
place of a smell there was a sound.    There was
something moving within.    Our John could
restrain himself no longer.    Seizing the handle
of the dish-cover, he raised it.    Beneath he saw
a clean and empty dish!    But stay—'twas not
empty; for, upon the verge of it, gathered
up in fright, cowered a mouse,—which had previously been running round and round within
the cover in a vain endeavour to escape.

Apprehending the nature of the trap which had
been laid for him, John Buncle now anxiously
sought to replace the lid as it had been.    But he

was not quick enough; for the mouse, having speedily recovered herself, now sprang out of the dish, and scampering across the table, on to the floor, and along the wainscot, was quickly lost to view in the folds of some heavy hangings. At the same moment the door opened, and the master of the house appeared on the threshold of the dining-room.

Without his pausing to look beneath the dish-cover, a single glance in the stone-breaker's face sufficed to inform him how matters stood. Seeing which, the faintest of all possible smiles passed across his countenance, and stretching out his hand towards his visitor, he thus spoke.

"John Buncle, my brother! let me point the moral of this tale.—An hour or two ago, I was walking—alone with Nature, in the eye of heaven —in the first hallowed freshness and purity of a fair morning granted to us both from God. And, as I walked, I silently gave thanks for the blessings of life and health and happiness— the boons of spirit and of sense, and strove to bring my mortal mind for one hour into harmony with the divine. The happy quiet of my orisons was broken by your voice." The speaker paused, and then resumed. "Profane swearing is, with you, a trick more than a vice. Evil is not meant, yet evil is spoken,—it is not in the heart, why is it on the lips?"

Here the Epicurean Philosopher, or Deipno-
sophist, paused again, and John hung his head,
like a schoolboy caught in the act.

"But that is not all.  A man of your shrewd-
ness, John, will have seen, long ere this, that, if
Adam yielded to temptation, there are others
who, placed in a similar situation and subjected
to a similar trial, would have acted precisely as
he did.  Nay, there are some who would seem
to combine the curiosity of Eve with the pliancy
of our Common Father.  Learn, therefore, to
bear without grumbling, or blaming others, such
trials as may fall to your lot; and refrain from
judging, or you yourself may chance to be
judged."

John, who still looked on the ground, shifted
a foot, but uttered nothing.  The Philosopher
resumed.

"Finally, learn this also,—that Adam's curse
conceals a blessing.  Ay, believe me, friend
John, there are worse ills in life than to *eat your
bread in the sweat of your face.*  Health, with
sound sleep o' nights, hearty appetite, and a
quiet mind, are compensations which have turned
Adam's bane to *our* happiness!—And now, go
back to your work; and as you break your
stones, reflect upon these my words."

As he spoke, the old gentleman's tone was
grave, yet from his eye there beamed a kindly
sympathy; for he knew that no philosopher who

is without an infinite tolerance for the petty
failings of a weak humanity can be worthy of
that honourable name. And when he had in
person conducted John Buncle to the door, and
taken his leave of him, there remained in the fist
of the latter a golden guinea.

John returned to his work. But whether the
lesson in wisdom which he had received was so
taken to heart as to lead him to amend his ways,
and so reduce the number of those surface faults
which had hitherto kept back a man who at the
core was sound and true from advancing in the
world,—this, *deponent sayeth not.**

* The outline of this rustic fable, or moral tale, was
narrated to me by George Dixon, a hedger in my employment. The narrator does not know its origin, but speaks
of it as a very old story, which has been familiar to him
all his life. It may possibly have been written down
before ; but I have not myself seen it in print.—G. D.

# A DARK PAGE FROM A FAMILY
# HISTORY.

THE friendship which subsisted between Lord
Bewcastle and Sir Ralph Gorrinberry was well
known throughout that part of Cumberland in
which they lived. It was matter of remark the
more, in that the Earl was young, spirited, and
self-willed, whilst the baronet was aged and
infirm, and of a querulous temper,—so that it
naturally seemed to the world at large that the
friends could have very little in common.
Nevertheless his lordship was unremitting in
his attentions to Sir Ralph, and a very frequent
visitor at his house.

Sir Ralph Gorrinberry's life had been spent
in the public service, in which he had held more
than one high appointment. He had seen men
and cities, sovereigns, camps, and courts. He
had been blessed with good natural powers of
observation, and had developed a certain acid,
cynical wit, which made him, on occasion—when
his gout was not too troublesome—a very
entertaining companion. After leading the life

of a man of pleasure until age had compelled him to abandon the *rôle*, he had contracted a marriage with a handsome young woman of obscure family ; who, when she became his wife, having youth and strength upon her side, was reported to rule him, and to do so with a rule which was not by any means too gentle.

At length the old diplomatist succumbed to his many infirmities, and the countryside was not surprised when, after a decent interval, his widow became Countess of Bewcastle. Sir Ralph had had no children ; but, by her second husband, the Countess became the mother of one daughter. This child, who had been christened Ruth, was from her earliest years her father's idol. And, apart from a father's passion for an only child, she was certainly a strangely attractive little mortal. Of diminutive proportions and of a delicate beauty, she the more astonished those who saw her for the first time by the fairy-like quickness of her wit. The dominant characteristic of her disposition was a winning, affectionate playfulness. With her father she simply did what she pleased.

In course of time, whilst still in middle life, the Countess (who was several years older than her second husband) died, and father and daughter were left alone together. Lady Ruth was now growing up ; but the lowness of her stature, the easy happiness of her experience in life, left her still in outward appearance, as in many other respects, a child. It was about this time that Lord Bewcastle introduced into the house a young man a few years older than Ruth, whose duties were to be those of secretary and librarian to his lordship. The Earl informed his daughter beforehand that Francis Damory was the only son of an old friend of his. He had been left an orphan, in poor circumstances, at a tender age, and his education had been at Lord Bewcastle's expense. Lady Ruth felt her sympathies aroused by this description, and when she came to see the librarian face to face these sympathies received no check. In character and appearance, Damory was the perfect incarnation of an epithet once much in vogue among novelists, but which would now be voted *démodé*,—the epithet "interesting." His handsome features, his gentle manners, his reserve, his melancholy, were precisely such as were calculated to appeal to the romantic imagination of the age in which he lived. But it was not in externals only that he merited commendation, being in reality a high-minded youth, and one who cultivated, amid loneliness and sadness, a secret practice of virtue and honour. He was, furthermore, a student of some elegance; whilst a certain air of mystery which hung about him by no means diminished the unconscious fascination which he exercised.

Lord Bewcastle was disposed to treat him
kindly; but he encountered unexpected difficulty
in winning the confidence of one whose life, so
far, had left him acquainted with little of
sympathy.

The post of librarian and secretary at Bewcastle was not one of onerous duties. The Earl
was devoted to the pleasures of the chase, and
regarded not that fair tradition which, in its
delineation of ideal manhood, hung the lyre
beside the bow and quiver. His letters, which
were few in number, were short and to the
point; and he seldom entered his library.
It thus happened that the librarian found
much of his time thrown upon his hands. He
was, also, himself thrown much into the society
of his patron's daughter. Since his arrival at
the Castle, Lady Ruth had, indeed, shown
signs of developing a somewhat studious turn.
As one who had always had her own way, she
had as a child been suffered to some extent to
neglect her studies ; but now, as she grew older—
so she, in a conversation, informed the librarian
—she began to see the importance of remedying
those defects in her education which had resulted
from early light-mindedness. The young man,
who probably felt that his liberal salary was
being too easily earned, declared in reply that
nothing in the world would afford him greater
satisfaction than to do what might be in his

power to forward her ladyship's studies.  Ruth
thanked him very sweetly for his kind offer,
and said that she would take him at his word.
And so she did.   And thus, day after day, as he
sat at work in the subdued light poured through
heraldic window-panes, in a recess of the library,
Lady Ruth would enter to him, bearing in her
arms some tome almost as big as herself, and
would join him in his researches.  She proved
a wonderfully apt pupil ; but she interrupted his
studies sorely.   He had agreed to teach her
Greek ; but, in exchange—without stipulation
made, and all for love—she taught him a lore of
which, poor fellow ! he was quite ignorant, yet
which is the one thing truly worth knowing in
the world.   For poets, indeed, may deal in
golden words ;  but every word—now arch, now
tender, now demure—which fell from those sweet
lips was to the finest gold what the living, blush-
ing, girl is to the statue.   The librarian was not
quite so dull-eyed a bookworm as Cousin Modus;
and even Modus masters this lesson in the end.

The affair had reached this stage when Lord
Bewcastle got wind of it.   A thing so unheard
of as that the secretary should dare to raise his
eyes to his employer's daughter had never entered
his lordship's mind; and he did not guess that
in this case the initiative had come from that
daughter herself.  He at once summoned Damory
to his presence, and summarily dismissed him

from the Castle. Poor Francis did not question
the justice of this treatment, though, to give him
his due, he had entered upon the path of love—
a captive led in flowery chains—almost without
reflection, most assuredly without design. He
now felt that all the brightness was gone out of
his life, and, greatly downcast, he began to make
his preparations for leaving Bewcastle.

He had intended to take his departure without
bidding farewell to Lady Ruth. Poor and obscure
as he was, he was not without a pride of his own;
and he must be forgiven if he told himself, in his
bitterness, that his absence would not long be
regretted. But, in so saying, he did his lady-love
grievous injustice. The news of her friend's
dismissal soon reached her, and at once all the
sympathy and generosity of a nature that was
singularly quick to feel was aroused and under
arms. Divining that the secretary's sense of
honour would lead him to leave the Castle without seeing her, she paused not to consider, but
herself took the initiative and found him. Now,
although the youthful couple had travelled some
days' journey along the path of love, no explicit
declaration, nor anything resembling it, had, so
far, passed between them. They were both of
them very young and inexperienced,—Lady
Ruth being but sixteen, and Damory barely
twenty. But now, in the tumult of grief and
indignation, what had been vaguely dreamed of,

hinted at, guessed, before, was in a moment made plain. The lovers wept together, and Lady Ruth consoled.

But her nature was not one to accept an unwelcome situation without a struggle to improve it. So, when she and her lover had mingled their tears and bitter-sweet consolations for a time, she set her nimble brain to work to see if nothing could be done to alleviate their distress. And, sure enough, in a very few moments, she had devised an ingenious plan, which she proceeded to communicate to Francis. It was bold, it was daring, it was difficult; but Ruth Delaval had inherited a share of her father's spirit, and she was not one to stick at difficulty or danger. With Damory it was different. He had scruples where she had none; and perhaps the hardest part of the task she had set herself lay in overcoming these scruples. However, Damory, though high-minded, was but mortal; and who that was not more than mortal could have resisted the persuasions, the arguments with so good a show of reason, now employed by such a girl as Lady Ruth? In fine, he allowed himself to be convinced, and it was arranged between them that her plan should be put into execution.

At the stated hour, the secretary took his leave of the Castle for ever. In the course of the afternoon Lord Bewcastle and his daughter met, and his lordship was pleased to observe that

Ruth's manner, if graver than usual, was perfectly composed, and that she made no reproachful allusion to the incident of the morning. The Earl thought he knew womankind, or at least knew his own daughter whom he so dearly loved,—a delusion into which men of the simpler sort and others not seldom fall.

Towards nightfall his lordship was informed that Lady Ruth had not come in from her walk. His fears were at once aroused in a degree which struck the bystanders as being out of all proportion with the trifling nature of the cause. Inquiries were immediately set on foot, and sure enough information was in time elicited that at a late hour in the afternoon a cloaked and hooded female figure of diminutive stature had been observed to enter a strange carriage, which was drawn up outside the park wall at a point where there was a postern gate. The carriage had, thereupon, driven rapidly away.

"In which direction did it drive?" inquired his lordship, almost suffocated as it seemed by rage, or by some other feeling.

"Toward the setting sun, my lord."

"By heaven! Then the villain has entrapped my child, and they have fled to Gretna Green."

Whatever the lamentable deficiencies of his speculative powers, the Earl was a man of prompt and decisive action. Without losing a moment, he ordered his carriage-and-four to be

brought to the door, and taking two or three
attendants with him, and charging the coachman
to drive for his life, he set off in pursuit of the
fugitives. The last remains of daylight were
fading from the sky as they left behind them the
desolate region known as Spadeadam Waste.
Driving at full gallop wherever the road would
admit of it, they crossed the Roman Road and
emerged upon the high moors. Veiled in the
darkness to their left, lay the lovely and extensive
panorama which, from this point of view, is presented by the Vale of the Irthing.

"They cannot have much more than a couple
of hours' start of us," muttered the Earl, "and
we have four horses to their two."

Then he relapsed once more into his sombre
reverie, in the corner of the carriage, and only
spoke when he had orders to give. But from the
twitching of his hands, from the passion which
he betrayed when an unavoidable delay occurred,
the servants could judge how intense was the
impatience which consumed their ordinarily im-
perturbable master.

The distance to be traversed was not much
more than about twenty miles ; but, despite the
speed to which the horses were lashed whenever
it was possible, the inequalities of the road
rendered progress comparatively slow. A good
deal of time was also lost in making inquiries at
lonely wayside cottages. For the cottagers had

generally been bribed to silence by the fugitives ;
and, though a larger bribe untied their tongues,
they were so long in answering to the Earl's
summons—pretending to be slumbering heavily
—that he soon made shift to dispense with their
information, and directed his servants to push
on without pause for Gretna. There was no
opportunity on this cross-country road of ob-
taining fresh horses until they reached Long-
town, by which time they were so near their
destination as to make a change not worth
while.

They were now upon comparatively level
ground ; and, jaded though the horses were,
the travelling-carriage flew along at a terrific
rate. The night was of an almost sensible
darkness ; and the momentarily-illumined leafy
boughs of trees swept the windows of the carriage as it swayed in its mad career. For, ever
and anon, the Earl kept shouting to his men to
make yet greater speed. At last the river Sark
was crossed, and the village passed, and the
Marriage House stood before them. There were
no lights in its windows. Dashing up the short
approach to the house, the carriage drew up
before it, and Lord Bewcastle and his servants,
alighting, thundered on the door. No answer
came to their summons. Still and dark, the
house seemed like a mansion of the dead.

"This is all of a piece with their knavery ! "

cried the exasperated nobleman to his companions. " By God, if the door's not opened to
me in a minute, I swear I'll have ye break it in !"

One of the men took a lamp from the carriage,
and by its light examined the gravel.

"They have not left the house," said he,
returning from his inspection, "unless they've
done it afoot. Them's the wheel-marks of the
brisky, and they lead to the stables and no
farther."

At last the sound of footsteps advancing over
the flagged passage inside came to their ears.
The bolt was withdrawn, and the door was
opened by the landlord in his nightcap. Without paying the slightest attention to the man's
acted astonishment, the Earl and his followers
pushed their way without ceremony into the
house, and began to search it. The ground-floor
rooms were dark and deserted; but in one of
them the remains of a repast laid for two
attracted the attention of the searchers. Several
emptied glasses stood round about, as if a toast
had been drunk. Uttering a frightful imprecation, Lord Bewcastle snatched a light and
rushed upstairs. The attendants followed, with
plenty of clatter and tramping. As they reached
the landing, a door at the end of the passage
opened, and the secretary stood before them.
Instead of falling upon him with violence, or
storming at him, as the servants had expected,

the Earl grasped him breathlessly by the arm, and led him into a side room. There the two remained closeted together for some minutes. At the end of that time, the secretary passed out of the room once more. He bore no marks of bodily harm, yet so altered in appearance was he that the onlookers in the passage scarcely recognised him. A moment later Lady Ruth joined her father. She was lightly attired in a white *demi-toilette*, her hands were clasped before her, and flitting forward she flung herself upon her knees at Lord Bewcastle's side, in the attitude of the Penitent imploring forgiveness. But on her face all the time there was a demure expression of fun just kept in check and ready to break forth at any moment,—as though she well knew that the situation was not in reality serious, and that the forgiveness she pleaded for would not be very hard to win. For by such means as these she had always been accustomed hitherto to surmount the difficulties of life. But, for the first time in her experience, the Earl turned away his head from her pretty acting, and sobbed and groaned aloud.

" Father ! " she exclaimed, in the extremity of astonishment ; for the breaking down of the robust and masterful Earl was to her as if the hills had moved.

At the same moment an exclamation came from the adjoining room which startled them

7

both. Animated by one impulse, they rushed
to the door of communication. But the Earl,
who was first, stopped short when he reached
the door, and held his daughter back from entering. For there, upon the bed, in the very article
of death, he had beheld the form of Francis
Damory. In his throat there was a ghastly,
self-dealt wound. His sensitive mind had
proved unable to support the terrible sorrow
and dishonour which, through no fault of his
own, had fallen suddenly upon him; and finding
himself placed in a situation scarcely less awful
than that which the toils of circumstance had
prepared for Laius' son, he had acted even more
rashly than did the King of Thebes in the
tragedy.

.    .    .    .    .    .

From that day, the fair, the joyous, the loving
Lady Ruth appeared no more in the world's
eye. The remaining years of her life were
passed in strict seclusion at Bewcastle ; and—
her beauty, her gaiety, her womanhood, frosted
in the bud, beyond all hope of recovery—it was
not long ere she herself was laid in the last cold
sleep. Her father, a changed man, did not
survive her long. On his death, the title and
estate passed to a kinsman. But the new peer
did not take up his abode at Bewcastle. The
house was closed, and all but two of the servants
were dismissed. These two, a middle-aged man

and his wife, were known to receive unusually
high wages. But they kept themselves strictly
to themselves, and admitted no visitors except
the clergyman, who called to see them about
once every three months. So close, indeed, was
their seclusion, that—those being the days of
superstition—the Castle in time acquired the
reputation of being haunted,—poachers and
peasants who had crossed the park at late hours
declaring that they had seen lights moving in
the upper storeys of the house, whilst the care-
taker and his wife were known to inhabit the
basement. There were even some who further
affirmed that they had heard inexplicable cries.
But if inquisitive persons sought to satisfy their
curiosity as to these matters, they never received
any encouragement from the care-taker, his wife,
or the parson.

Well, years passed, and still the lord of
Bewcastle did not visit his domain, still the
exclusiveness at the Castle was not relaxed. In
the fulness of time the care-taker's wife died,
then the care-taker himself died, and then the
parson. But they were followed by successors
in no wise less inscrutable than they themselves
had been. In this manner many years went by,
during which the Castle had no history, or at
least no history that was ever known. There
were even several Earls in succession who had
never looked on the estate from which they took

their name.    At last—some four-score years
after the date of the runaway marriage—in
consequence of intelligence which had been
imparted to him, the Lord Bewcastle of the day
paid Bewcastle a visit.    After inspecting it, he
professed himself charmed with the wildness of
the park, and the lonely situation of the Castle,
high up upon the fells ; and, to the satisfaction
of the neighbourhood, he announced his intention of living there.    Accordingly some much-
needed repairs were executed, and the house
was to some extent modernised.    Whilst these
alterations were being made, stories of a blood-
stained floor and of a bricked-up room discovered by the workmen became current in the
district.    But when the Earl, accompanied by
the Countess and a large young family, arrived
upon the scene, such stories had to make way
for topics more attractive.    The new Earl was
of a lively and hospitable disposition, and
entertained upon a liberal scale ; so that the old
cheerful life of the Castle was quickly restored,
and the tradition of its having at one time been
haunted was mentioned only on winter's nights
when fireside tales are told.    And perhaps this
was well, for Lord Bewcastle and others of his
family were always somewhat disconcerted when
such references were made in their presence.

# THE POT OF GOLD.

IF popular tales are to be believed, there are
many buried treasures hidden in the Border
Land. One such treasure, for instance, is described as lying somewhere in the Cheviot Hills.
The story is that it was concealed by two
brothers in time of war; that it is wrapt in a
bullock's hide; and that it lies exactly midway
between two places—only one of which, unfortunately, is specified. A second treasure is more
particularly localised, for the very field in which
it is concealed is known. Yet this knowledge
must not be turned to account. For when, years
ago, some countrymen set spade in the earth to
dig for it, we are told that the heavens presently
grew dark and that a flash of forked lightning
was seen, whilst an angry muttering of thunder
overhead seemed to warn the treasure-seekers at
their peril to desist from a labour which was
displeasing to Heaven. Again, at Pennymuir,
somewhere close to Agricola's Camp, there lies
buried the body of the English Knight whom
Jock of Heavyside slew. He is known to have

been interred clad in his silver armour, and his remains would therefore make the fortune of any man who should chance to light upon them. Then there are, also, other treasures with which it would not be safe to meddle. These were buried in times of pestilence—perhaps as sacrifices, to propitiate some Unknown Power—and were they to be unearthed, the plague, it is said, would break out again.

Readers may think what they please of such stories as these; but, as if to prevent their falling into entire discredit, it does actually happen that, once in many years, a buried treasure is discovered. Some years ago there was an instance of this in Berwickshire,—when a farm-labourer, whilst ploughing, turned up an antique urn containing a deposit of gold coins. This occurrence was soon noised abroad, and it sufficed to give a new lease of life to all the old fables of buried treasures ever current in the Border Land, and to raise hopes and dreams of a like stroke of good fortune in countless heads and hearts within a circuit of many miles.

In those days, there was living at Whinny, between Morebattle and Oxnam, an elderly labouring man, William Wastle by name. Now Wastle fills no space in the world's history. In all his days he was not known over more than a square mile or two of country, nor to more than at most a few score of his fellow-creatures.

Yet, notwithstanding, Willie was certainly the possessor of some of the qualities which go to the making of a great man.   He had the busiest, the most subtle, of brains; and he was "original." He did not follow other people's lead, that is, like one in a flock of sheep,—he took a line of his own: he had a way of his own of doing the commonest things.   For instance, in his very early days when he drove a pair of horses, he would not stop them, as the other ploughmen did, by shouting Woa-hoa! but simply by saying S-st.   (This method of procedure he considered much more refined, in case his master should be present.)   The above is only one small instance of the originality of his ways.   But his appearance, his dress, and his simplest acts were also characteristic.   His small wiry form, his acute puckered countenance, and his little bright eyes half hidden under bushy eyebrows, were unmistakable.   Then he had introduced the variation upon "Nature's simplest habit," the "kersacky," of a voluminous black gravat, and thus attired he would go about his business, with his head bent, and with an air as if he were intent upon the execution of some clever, silently-matured plan,—which, indeed, he often was.   In short, in the language of the people round about, Willie Wastle was "a character."

Well, at the least, Willie had achieved one success which the proverb informs us is denied

to most great men,—he was a hero to the two
persons in the world who knew him best,
namely, to his wife, Jannie, and to his neighbour,
Jimmy Fair,—two simple creatures who never
tired in their admiration of his ways, his notions,
and his speeches. James and Willie were
drainers to trade, and worked together. James
Fair, otherwise called Jimmy the Divot, was
a tall man of substantial form, good at "taking
out the second spading." In a general way
he had not much to say for himself, but would
be content with repeating "Most re-*mark*-able,"
and things like that, in the pauses of Willie's
speech. He was Willie's Achates, and was
generally to be seen following him wherever
he went, a step and a half behind. When not
thus escorted, Willie—like other great men of a
certain class—was almost always alone.

Willie, alas! was not a man of education.
Had he been so, his keen and active mind might
have raised him in the world. Yet, on second
thoughts, I am wrong to cry alas! for my hero
did not believe in education. He believed in
mother-wit. Education, even in his day, had
spoilt the rising generation. And what need
had he of book-learning when, by the consent of
Jannie and Jimmy, Nature herself had made
him "a jaynus"?

He had no family. His mind imperatively
demanded something to wreak its energy upon,

and the consequence was that he was always very much taken up with one hobby or another. In the words of the outside world, he was "awfully maggotive." And his genius was speculative rather than practical, delighting in the abstract, in theories, and in visions of what things might be.

Now it so happened that the story of the Berwickshire farm-servant's treasure-trove, together with all the talk to which it gave rise, came to Willie's ears. It made a deep impression upon him; and, in short, the little man became bitten with the treasure-seeker's mania. Gossip had magnified the value of the find; and, to Willie's busy unenlightened mind, the truth that what man has done man may do presented itself as bearing with special relevancy upon this matter as it had regard to himself. He knew vaguely that the neighbourhood in which he lived and worked was supposed to abound in traces of an unnamed people who had long since passed away. Again, his trade as a drainer led him daily down into the bowels of the earth— the very kingdom, or world, of hidden treasures. Why might not he, as well as another man, be so far blessed as to light one day upon some store of alien, long-concealed, wealth? He had worked hard all his life, and he deserved, if any man did, to end his days in ease and comfort. (You see the consideration of deserts still enters into

a poor man's calculation when he speculates as
to the future.)   But ease and comfort alone were
by no means enough to satisfy the aspirations of
the soaring soul of the goodman of Whinny.
His luxuriant imagination revelled in dreams of
barbaric magnificence and of insolent expenditure.   He decided that his Jannie should wear
a golden gown, and that he himself would loll
in perfect idleness, with servants within call, to
fetch him a drink of water, or a nip of whisky,
when he needed it.   At last, by dint of con-
tinually dwelling on it, the thought of finding a
treasure became a fixed idea in Willie's mind.
He mused on it by day ; and, what was much
more remarkable, at last he dreamed of it by
night.   Even so, as old Theocritus observes,
do sleeping dogs scent meat.   I believe that
working-men, as a rule, are exempt from
dreams ; and drainers, who are the hardest-
wrought of working-men, ought to be especially
exempt from them.   Yet, nevertheless, one night,
as Willie lay beside his old Jannie in the darkness of their cottage—the stillness broken only
by the ticking of the eight-day clock—he
dreamed that he was working with Jimmy in a
drain, as he did every day.   He struck a blow
with his pickaxe,—and then, all at once, the
earth gave way and opened, and the next
moment he found himself alone in a lofty
vaulted chamber.   Some indistinctness and

confusion followed ; but the upshot of it all was
that a minute later he was shouting aloud to
Jimmy, and handing out the yellow gold to him
by "nieviefu's," nay by "gowpens!" From this
time forth Willie Wastle held the belief that he
was destined to find a treasure.

Only believe firmly that you are destined for
great things and you will find it will come true.
So was it with the man of Whinny. For a long
time after he had dreamed his dream, nothing
of any consequence happened. He continued,
as before, to live his life of toil and poverty,—
against which it had never occurred to him to
murmur ; but toil and poverty themselves were
illuminated and transfigured by the brilliancy of
his visions, say rather by the vividness of his ex-
pectations. He had long to wait ; but at last
the fated day arrived.

It happened one summer forenoon that Willie
and his mate, assisted by a tileman, were howking
a drain in a low-lying green field by the river
side, where there was some natural, or self-
sown, wood. The spot was close to Caphope, or
Cappoch,—where long afterwards the remains of
a Roman villa were discovered,—and the ground
bore traces of having been disturbed. The men
had paused to eat their "nacket," and were
about resuming work. Willie, attired in the
earth-coloured garb of his calling, already stood
in the bottom of the drain ; and, just as he had

done in his dream, he struck a blow with his pickaxe—as he had done many thousand times before. The loose soil rolled down into the cutting, and disclosed to view a strange, old-world, earthenware vase embedded in the clay. The astonished drainer tapped it with the tool that was in his hand, and it gave forth a metallic chink. Then, all at once, a degree of vertigo seized upon Wastle. It was accompanied by a singular sensation of having lived through the experience before. Pulling himself together, he scrambled out of the drain and looked about him. Yes! there was no mistaking it,—the scene was familiar. He recognised the daisied green which stretched before him in the sunlight, and the singular, spreading, half-uncovered, roots of a self-sown oak tree growing close at hand. It was the place where he had found the treasure in his dream! If he had had any doubts before, they were dispelled. This was the moment for which he had lived; and he recognised the necessity of rising to the occasion. Quickly collecting his scattered wits, therefore, he beckoned to Jimmy, who was not far off, led him forward without speaking, and silently impressing the necessity of silence upon him, pointed out the mysterious find. (The tile-man, Peter, all this time was still busy with his bread and cheese under the hedge, and this was as Willie would have it; for though Jimmy was his sworn crony, with whom he gladly shared his good fortune, the tileman was an outsider.) The Divot's slow comprehension did not grasp the situation at once. Then Willie solemnly tapped the vase again ; and again, as before, the metallic chink was heard. And then he began to make eager signs to Jimmy—still refraining from speaking lest the tileman should hear what he said. At last his meaning dawned on the bewildered Divot, who joyfully seizing his spade would have unearthed the vase forthwith. But Willie stayed his hand. Such simple and straightforward procedure in such a crisis was too rash. Now was the time, he felt, to prove himself a man apart.

"Man !" cried he in indignant remonstrance, "no anither chap ! no anither chap as lang's ye live." And then, recollecting himself, he added in a whisper, " Man, Jimmy ! your fortun's made."

It had not been for nothing that Willie had dwelt day and night, asleep and awake, on the prospect of finding a treasure. He knew—none better—the necessity of secrecy and precaution ; and already his swift and subtle brain had sketched out a plan of action to suit the present critical circumstances. Whilst the tileman still sat munching contentedly, he proceeded to cover up the vase carefully with earth as it had been before ; and when the former returned to his work, he informed him with the most natural

air of unconcern in the world that he might
"tile up," and that his services would not be
wanted any more just now, for that he (Willie)
and his mate did not intend to work any more
that day.

Leaving their tools, the two labourers then
walked home together; and, as they went, Willie
explained the nature of his ruse for preventing the
tileman from sharing in their find. The simple
Jimmy was at first inclined to regard their good
fortune as problematical. He had certainly seen
an urn; but what sure proof had he that it was
filled with gold? Willie, however, had no tolerance for such creeping, rule-of-thumb logic. He
would not listen to the expression of his companion's doubts; besides, was there not the
proof of the metallic chink? So the feeble
objections of the Divot—who was generally
accustomed to place implicit confidence in the
dicta of his more gifted work-mate—were over-
ruled, and he was silenced. Meantime the
treasure-finder trod on air. He felt that he had
wrought his last day's work as a labourer.

The cronies inhabited a whinstone double
cottage, which stood by itself—apart from other
dwellings—by the side of the road which leads
from Oxnam to Morebattle. Now it so happened that at this time their wives—though
they lived side by side and had no other neighbours—had not spoken to each other for many

months. There was a quarrel of long standing between them, which had arisen in this way. Willie's wife, Janet, had a hare-lip; and she fancied that on one occasion she had caught Jimmy's wife (whom she had long suspected of looking down upon her) in the act of mimicking her way of speaking for the amusement of a chance caller. Jimmy's wife had a cutty temper and a scolding tongue; words had passed, and from that day forward—although their men were so "chief," and though Jannie, as she expressed it, could do well enough with Jimmy—there had been no further dealings between the two solitary women.

But now, when the great news of the discovery was communicated, bygones were forgotten, and the surprise and joy of the women broke the silence of many days. And—as secrecy was of the first importance, and they could not possibly talk the matter over standing each by her own door-cheek—before Jannie well knew where she was, she had followed her husband and actually stood in Mistress Fair's cottage. What a discussion then began! A storm of questions from the women assailed Willie; but it pleased him to assume a knowing, tantalising reserve. However, as he was both the finder of the treasure and the master-mind of the party, it was an understood thing that the conduct of this delicate piece of business should rest entirely in his hands.

Then Jimmy's wife, with a smirk, produced a bottle of whisky; and they "tasted" all round, in celebration of the glorious event. And then, in course of time, the men separated; but the women remained together, the fastest and most effusive of friends.

Willie Wastle put his hands behind his back and sauntered off by himself, to mature his plans in solitude. Toward nightfall he returned; and any observer might have gathered from his countenance that his scheme of action was complete. The others came together to hear it revealed; and this time it was in Jannie's house that the conclave met. A lighted candle was set in the centre of a small deal table,—around which, facing each other, the four simple souls took seats. Then Jannie got up again, to see that there was nobody listening outside. The light of the smoking candle glittered upon Willie's eyes, which were brimful of meaning, and shone upon the broad shoulders and fixed gaze of Jimmy the Divot, upon Jannie's up-looking contorted features, and upon the arms of Mrs. Fair, which rested on the table rolled in her apron. Then, marking his words as he spoke with appropriate movements of his forefinger, the good man of Whinny unfolded his plan. He spoke in a conspirator's whisper, and the four heads bent closer together to catch his words.

The plan was briefly as follows. At a little before midnight, the speaker and Jimmy were to take a lantern and to repair to the scene of their find, to lift the treasure. Meantime the women were to pack up such of their worldly goods as were easily portable, and to place them in Jimmy's cart to be ready for immediate flight. Flight, as Willie explained, was an absolutely necessary measure. For how could they hope to live on at Whinny and enjoy their remodelled existence (which would make a stir in the country), without exciting the suspicions of Gover'ment? And if once that vaguely-defined power got wind of their luck, it would not fail to appear on the scene in some corporate shape or other, and forcibly deprive them of their gains. No—they could not stay at home; America was the place for them. They would be beyond the reach of Gover'ment there. Now, it is a fact that not one of these honest creatures would have stolen so much as a pin from a neighbour. But their conception of justice was a larger one than that embodied in the Law of the Land; and, in defrauding the Government of ten thousand pounds or so—for at such a sum they roughly estimated the treasure,—they felt that they were simply appropriating what was their own by right, and doing no person any ill.

As soon as the treasure should be safely

8

stowed away in the cart, the fugitives were
themselves to mount, and at the best speed of
Jimmy's sorry jade to make for Leith. The
details of the journey they perforce left vague;
for they were none of them travellers. However, the essential thing was that, at the sea-port,
a vessel would be waiting to convey them across
the Atlantic. And, once in the States, the world
would be at their feet, and they would enter
upon a life of pleasure and idleness of which
Willie drew a glowing picture. The others
added details at their pleasure, and in this
agreeable occupation the minutes were consumed till it was time for the men to set out on
their momentous errand.

These then sallied noiselessly forth — the
women shading the candle-flame at the open
door as they wished their husbands good speed.
There was no moon. The summer night was
dark, and the air heavy. A horn lantern, which
was to light their labours, hung down from
Willie's hand. Proceeding on their way, they
were somewhat surprised to find, when they
reached the house where the tileman and his
family dwelt, that there was a light burning
in it.

"What can they be doing wi' a light at this
time o' night?" inquired Wastle rather uneasily.

"Maybe there's someone no weel," was Jimmy's
matter-of-fact reply.

They trudged on, up hill and down dale,—at times pausing to listen, to make sure that they were not followed, and then pushing on once more. At last they reached the meadow where, beneath the green sod—like a pearl asleep in the depths of ocean—lay the hidden wealth which was to transform their lives. Willie set down the lantern on the loosened soil which had been flung out of the drain, and cautiously unveiled it. Its light illuminated the wheeling-board, a barrow lying near upon its side, and a heap of pink tiles; and so spread away over the trodden clay and the sward beyond. The tools lay where they had been flung down in the morning. Then the two old men leapt into the drain, and fell feverishly to their work. Trembling lest they should discover that the pot had in some mysterious manner melted or vanished during their absence, they undid the last labours of the morning. The soil rolled down before their spades, and presently the red earthenware side of the urn was uncovered. With a gasp of relief, Willie tapped upon it—as he had already done twice before. The pot gave forth a hollow sound; but the old man's ear did not detect the metallic chink which it had noted, or fancied, in the fore part of the day. However, in his present eagerness, this did not trouble him. Carefully loosening the soil, the two quaint delvers now with some labour released the jar from its

prison of a thousand years. Then Willie stepped
forward to raise the lid. The soul—the wealth
concealed within—was now to be set free from
its living tomb,—whence, like some comet—an
embodied joy—it should fly away on golden
wings into the uttermost parts of the earth,
bearing behind it, hanging to its tail, four
homely, oddly-assorted, laborious, simple beings.
Grasping the top-piece, Willie lifted the lid—and
straightway, like a dream, his golden illusion
was dispelled. The pot was empty.

I pass lightly over the mournful and lingering
return of the treasure-finders to their home. In
the act of scaling the seventh heaven, Willie had
found himself pitchforked headlong back to the
common earth. Not only had his treasure
melted, not only was his hope dead (for such
discoveries are not made twice in a lifetime),
but his reputation as a "jaynus" had, as he
dimly felt, received a wound from which it
would never recover. Jimmy's woes were of a
homelier kind. His even nature had been less
lifted up than Willie's, and he had now not so
far to fall. Yet, as they walked home side by
side, his pace was even slower than his comrade's,
his mien was the more disconsolate ; for well he
guessed the skelping which awaited him when
his wife should learn how she had been fooled.

Meantime, some clouds having lifted, the
night had grown less dark, so that as the men

THE POT OF GOLD.—P. 116.

*New Border Tales.*]

approached the cottages, their wives—now resting after their labours—descried them afar off. Jannie expressed surprise at the slowness of their advance; but this, Jimmy's wife, with a good show of reason, attributed to the weight of the treasure which they carried. The husbands, on the other hand, when at last they came up, were astonished at the rapidity with which the women had laboured during their absence. The cottages seemed in that short time to have been entirely stripped and dismantled. The doors were locked on the outside; and Jannie, in her best bonnet and Paisley shawl, with a bundle on her knee, was seated on her corded trunk by the door-stone. And, as the men confronted her, stammering and shamefast, making pitiful efforts to pass the whole matter off as a joke, a noise of wheels was heard, and Mistress Fair, seated upon the top of the loaded cart, drove round from the stable behind the houses. It was evident that the women had truly done their part, and that they had shown a spirited determination that no time should be lost through their fault.

Surely we need not dwell upon the scene which followed? The just ire felt by Mrs. Fair when she found that she had had all her trouble for nothing was increased, not diminished, by the feeble and unlucky attempt made by the men to pass the disappointment off as a joke. The tempest of her wrath enveloped not only him who was her lawful property, but her neighbour's husband as well; and glad indeed was Willie to escape into his house and shut the door behind him. But for the ill-starred Jimmy there was no escape. And so, through the partition wall of the cottage, his wife's tongue could be heard wagging, furiously and incessantly, till the summer morning broke. Then the crestfallen workmen arose—to betake themselves to that laborious task to which they felt that they were now doomed, without hope of intermission, for as long as life, or strength, should hold out.

But this is not the end of my story. A few months after the events recounted above, it happened that Mistress Fair, leaving the old tavern called the Hottle, at Oxnam, encountered the tileman's daughter. The matron civilly gave the time of day; but the young woman responded by tossing her head, and in other ways displaying so much pride that Jimmy's wife was severely incensed. This was not all. When another few months had gone by, the tileman, accompanied by his family, unexpectedly left the neighbourhood. It was reported that they had gone abroad; and, sure enough, in course of time, a letter addressed by the afore-mentioned daughter to a friend in the neighbourhood, and bearing a foreign postmark, was received.

This letter contained many allusions to the altered and improved circumstances in which the writer and her family now lived,—a change which she declared that they owed to a legacy, inherited from a distant relative who had long been resident abroad.   Now, nobody remembered ever to have heard the tileman, or any one of his family (who, nevertheless, were not inclined to hide their light under a bushel), allude to any such relative.   These circumstances, therefore, when they were known, went far, in his own little coterie, to re-establish Willie's credit.   So he began to hatch maggots again just as industriously as ever before.   And, in reference to the treasure, to his dying day he was always accustomed to assert that the sound emitted by the jar when he had tapped it at midnight was of a completely different character to that which had greeted his ears when he had tapped it first.   But if Mistress Fair happened to be present, and to revert, as she generally did, to the fatal consequences of being too clever by half—to which she attributed the fact of the treasure having slipped through their fingers— the little man would thereupon at once grow silent and abashed.

# THE NABOB.

A STORY OF A "SCOTCH MARRIAGE."

MARGARET ——, the daughter of a well-to-do
tenant-farmer, in Selkirkshire, was beautiful and
self-willed. She had lost her mother early. Her
father—though she was his only child—was not
the man to spoil her; and, indeed, her growing up
had been attended by a considerable and ever-
increasing amount of friction between them. At
last matters reached a climax. In the absence of
an admirer in her own station in life, Margaret had
smiled upon the admiration eloquently expressed
in the eye of a handsome young servant on her
father's farm. Meetings took place between the
youthful couple; the man, poor fellow, lost his
head; and even Margaret, in her inexperience, had
the simplicity to seek an interview with her parent,
and to inform him that she was sure she should
never love any man but Robin, and that she
was ready to give everything to become his wife.
This was preposterous. The farmer stormed;
Margaret was placed in strict confinement in
her bedroom, on a diet of bread and water; and

the next rising sun beheld the sad figure of the young ploughman, bearing the little bundle which contained his all, betake himself across the fields, in the direction of the distant village where his home was.

When released from her imprisonment, as in due course she was, Margaret's temper was none of the sweetest, or most submissive. For many days no speech was exchanged between herself and her father. It was in this frame of mind that, as she was loitering one morning in the neighbouring fields, she was accosted by a gentleman on horseback in the prime of life, who asked her some simple question. Her negligent reply, the mingled *hauteur* and discontent of her demeanour, and, above all, her beauty, appeared to strike the stranger, whoever he might be, and he artfully prolonged the conversation—which Margaret, out of sheer indifference, allowed him to do. She would have thought no more of the incident, but, a few days afterwards, chancing to pass the same spot at nearly the same hour, she again saw the gentleman on horseback, who this time raised his hat and greeted her. Furthermore, in the course of the remarks which they exchanged, he somehow managed to inform her, without seeming to do so, that their meeting, in so far as he was concerned, was not due to accident, and that he had visited the spot daily at that hour since the day of their previous interview.

Margaret would not have been a woman if her curiosity had not been piqued, and she now took some trouble to determine the identity of her new acquaintance. Somewhat to her surprise, she discovered that he was no other than a man whose name she had of late very often heard mentioned, but in whose affairs, being preoccupied with her own, she had taken no interest.

Dixon Mather—or, as in accordance with the usage of those days he had recently been nicknamed, "The Nabob"—after starting from a very small beginning, had acquired a large fortune in the East India Company's service. He was a native of the district (though he had left it at an early age); and, as was known to one or two, was descended from an old, but long-impoverished, local family. But, being remembered chiefly, where he was remembered at all, as a threadbare little lad, the son of parents in a small way of business, it had come about that—notwithstanding that an estate which he had recently purchased had been a former property of his family—he had been viewed since his arrival in the neighbourhood, not in the light, so to speak, of a king come to his own again, but in that of a common *parvenu*. Now, it so happened that, at the time of which I am writing, this was a bitter and ever-present grievance to him. The exclusiveness of Scottish country

society in those days (and even in much later
ones) can to-day be scarcely realised by any one
who, in default of direct experience, has not had
minute information, at first hand, regarding it.
It was nothing less than a heartless, if unconscious, form of tyranny,—by which the stranger,
the most proper object of our hospitality, and the
social inferior, whose just due is our choicest
courtesy, were transformed alike into pariahs.
The county families of Mather's county had not
even paid him the compliment of turning up
their noses at him. They had simply ignored
him, behaving exactly as if they did not know
that any such person existed—which, in many
individual instances, may even very possibly have
been the case. For exclusive society has this in
its favour, which to the outsider is a very aggra-
vating attribute—that it is beautifully sufficient
to its own needs and requirements. What made
matters worse was that the Nabob was a great
man in his own estimation—an opinion which
the state and power he had so long enjoyed
among the subject races of the East made not
only pardonable, but the only one natural.
There was a pathetic side, too, to what might
otherwise have been either simple gregariousness,
or else that in reality amiable weakness which is
called, too harshly, " snobbery."

Sundered from his friends at a tender age, the
youthful Dixon had set before him, as his earliest

aim, to grow fabulously rich, return to his native
country, take up the position which he had been
taught by his parents to believe was his by right
of descent, and make every one happy around
him.   Alas for these young dreams ! Sometimes
they come true ; but the dear ones in whose lives
alone their brightness could enjoy a frail, subject-
ive reality—these are no more ; and the dreamer
himself is changed.

Mather's was a character in which a grievance
found spacious harbour.  Virile in matters of
action, womanish in those of feeling, intensely
emotional beneath a calm and reserved exterior,
introspective, he had lived much alone, and in
the absence of correcting influences, his natural
tendencies had run to seed.  He suffered also
from an affection of the liver, the effect of the
Indian climate, which often made him moody and
depressed.  It must be added in fairness, too,
that, if he felt himself isolated, neglected, and
cold-shouldered upon his country estate, he had
in some measure himself to blame for it.  More
than one of the country gentlemen, his neighbours, had made preliminary inquiries about him ;
which inquiries, had the information they elicited
been satisfactory, would in all probability have
been followed up by advances.  But, being met
by rumours of certain unusual, eccentric, and
high-handed acts into which the Nabob, unaccustomed as he was to the ways and restraints of

civilisation, had been betrayed, these gentlemen had unanimously resolved to delay further action, until circumstances should have revealed somewhat more distinctly the character of this possibly questionable interloper. Had Mather been informed of the grounds of their hesitation, it is possible that his subsequent conduct might have been different. As it was, having no one else to please, he determined, in a temper of pique and dudgeon, at least to please himself, and by a precipitate act made haste to place himself at once and forever beyond the pale of county society.

The meetings between himself and Margaret were repeated. She found in them a distraction, and he a pleasure of another order. At last, when the first barriers of reserve had been broken down between them, he, one day, in a half-bantering mood, invited her " to come and stay with him." As evil chance would have it, the conversation from that point took a deeper tone, with the result that that night, with the recollection of her injuries still rankling in her breast, Margaret took the irrevocable step of leaving her father's house.

She had resided with the Nabob for some five years, and had borne him three children, when an event occurred to break the monotony of their lives. It was upon the eve of a general election. Party politics at that time ran especially high; from the extent of his means and of his property, the Nabob was an influential man in the locality; and, in short, the time seemed at last to have come when he could be no longer overlooked. Accordingly, in due course, to his no small gratification, a very courteously-worded, friendly letter arrived from the Earl of——,Lord Lieutenant of the county, and a member of His Majesty's ministry. The courteously-worded, friendly letter, coming after a neglect so long continued, might, to any one who knew more about politics in the mother-country, have seemed very like an electioneering dodge; but the Lord Lieutenant deservedly bore a very high character, not only for ability, but for conduct and manners as well, and this explanation did not even occur to the Nabob. Besides, his lordship's seat was remote, whilst he himself had been so much absent from it, attending to the affairs of the nation, that there was ample excuse for his not having called upon the new-comer. His letter expressed regret for the omission, and went on to say that the writer was seeking the earliest opportunity of repairing it. His engagements required his presence in Mather's locality upon a certain day in the following week; would Mather receive him under his roof for the night, thus affording him an opportunity of making his acquaintance? From a man who was far and away the greatest in the county, this was delicate flattery, and the Nabob chuckled as he pictured to himself the surprise and (he hoped) anger of the smaller county magnates when they heard of it. He at once wrote a suitable reply in the affirmative, and having done so, determined to give his guest a reception which should be worthy of himself and the occasion. Almost for the first time since he had taken up his residence in the country, he experienced the pleasure and pride of having riches at his command.

A servant upon whose judgment he could depend was at once despatched, post, to Glasgow. In due course he returned, but not, as he had gone, unaccompanied. Footmen, a coachman, grooms, and (most important of all) a man cook, came with him; and these were followed by three waggons, heavily laden. In the waggons were boxes containing liveries for the servants; some handsome fancy articles of furniture and plate; every imaginable delicacy for the table (the rich merchants of Glasgow, great diners, saw to its market being kept supplied in this respect); rare hot-house plants for decoration, for it was winter; jewellery and a choice of gowns for Margaret. The *cortège* travelled night and day, and reached the Nabob's on the morning of the expected visit. Then all was bustle; and, under able guidance, in a few hours the Nabob's residence stood transformed. Every trace of his somewhat hugger-mugger, if free, style of

living had disappeared; and in its place appeared
a style which was the model of decorum and
propriety.    A sumptuous dinner was cooking
below stairs, and a number of richly-liveried servants stood ready to conduct the service.    The
Nabob himself had had a hair-dresser, and had
attired himself in a fashion of quiet good taste.
He felt that his opportunity had come.    He was
clever enough, if they only gave him a chance!

Late on the afternoon of the short day, an
out-rider trotted smartly up the approach and
rang a thundering peal; and a few minutes later,
a carriage-and-four rolled up to the Nabob's
door.    The meeting between host and guest was
all that could be wished.    The kindliness, the
simplicity, and the natural dignity (entirely free
from pretentiousness) of his lordship's manner
quite won the Nabob's heart, and set him at his
ease, so that throughout the dinner (which passed
off without a hitch) he talked freely, well, and
with animation.    I always heard him spoken of
by the few who, years ago, remembered him, as
a man of strong mental power, and his long
experience of a country unknown to the Cabinet
Minister, but about which the latter was eager to
acquire information, supplied him with at least
one excellent topic.    Margaret, richly jewelled
and attired, occupied the foot of the table.    She
looked her best, but took no part in the conversation.    And it was only when his glance for

a moment rested upon her, that Lord ———'s benign countenance became troubled, and a cloud seemed to gather upon his aristocratic features. The truth was that he had that after-noon heard a sinister report, but had refused to believe it.

At last the dinner came to an end. The wine was placed on the table, Margaret retired, and the Nabob and the Lord Lieutenant were left alone. This was the moment to which Mr. Mather had looked forward. In the case of most of his neighbours, he would have felt that, for making a favourable impression, he might safely rely upon the unaided qualities of his excellent Madeira. But with his lordship it was different. He was a man who drank little; but he could appreciate good conversation, and accordingly his host had reserved his best and most telling stories for the last. Elated by his success—for, during the whole of dinner, whilst his conversation had been playing with such a brilliant, lambent, variable flame over so many subjects, he had never ceased to keenly watch its effect upon his guest—he was for the moment off his guard, as with a manner of less extreme deference than he had hitherto shown, he seated himself beside his lordship.

"What you were saying about paternal affec-tion, my lord, reminds me of a curious and touching incident which came under my own

9

observation when I was residing upon a remote station in the Madras Presidency."

So saying, Mather was about to fill the Lord Lieutenant's glass and his own, when, to his surprise and acute discomfiture, he received an unexpected check.

His lordship pushed back his chair.

" Excuse me, Mr. Mather, but before we enter upon indifferent matters, there is one serious question which I must put to you."

" I am at your lordship's service."

For a moment the Lord Lieutenant hesitated. Then he spoke out.

" The lady who sat at the foot of your table just now—is she your wife ? "

" She is not."

" But it is your intention, I hope, to make her your wife ? "

" No, my lord."

His lordship rose to his feet.

" Then, sir, I have been mistaken in my man," said he, curtly.    And with that he moved towards the bell and rang it.    When the servant appeared, he gave orders for his horses to be put to at once, and his carriage to come round to the door.

But, before taking his departure, he made an earnest and sincere appeal to Mr. Mather to right, in so far as still lay in his power, the wrong which he had done to Margaret.    He spoke feelingly of the sacredness of the family tie ; referred to the pretty, unoffending children (whom he had seen before dinner), who, through their father's selfishness, were destined to bear through life a branded name ; and, finally, appealed to his host, as to a man of sense and of the world, upon the useless folly of flying in the face of society. But he spoke to deaf ears. So long as all had gone smoothly and well, the Nabob had shown himself the pattern of polished affability; but now that things had taken another turn, winds and waves themselves were not more inexorable than he. His concealed, but in reality so highly sensitive, nature had received a harsh check ; and he now began to tingle with a sense of having betrayed subserviency, of having made himself ridiculous in his efforts to please his distinguished guest. And, as if to correct his error, he flew to an opposite extreme, maintained a harsh and obdurate demeanour, even when his heart was touched and his conscience pricked him, and, at last (as Lord —— reached his climax), reverting to the manners of recent years, sprang to his feet, and, swearing a great oath, declared that "the day on which he married Margaret should be the day of his death."

Lord —— knew human nature too well to waste further words on him in his present mood ; and, the carriage being at that moment announced, notwithstanding the lateness of the hour, he at once took his departure. As the sound of the carriage-wheels died away, Dixon Mather dropped back into his seat, and, resting his head upon his arms, and his arms on the table, sank into a reverie.

The prospect before him was gloomy. He felt that he had had his chance, and that, owing to a foolish error of his own, it had slipped through his fingers. His sin had found him out. His long-cherished hope of taking the position in the county to which, whether by delusion or not, he believed himself by descent entitled, passed from him forever; and, with the sad courage and wisdom which come to us when we have faced the worst, he smiled to think that he could ever have attached so much importance to such a bauble. Then his thoughts went back to old times; and the gentle sayings of his mother and his old father's cheery presages when he was leaving them (for the last time, as it proved) to go forth into the world to seek his fortune, came back and touched his heart to a long-unwonted softness. There stood between him and a new, wise, happy life, only one little never-to-be-surmounted "if." But he had made a mess of things, and he felt tired.

But he had other thoughts than for himself. Notwithstanding his impervious demeanour, the eloquent words of the Lord Lieutenant—

the man of stainless character, grown old in
honour, his own friend of an hour—had effected a
lodgment in spite of him, and their echo haunted
him now. He thought of Margaret. His fancy
for her had long ago passed off, and her life with
him during the past five years had been no bed
of roses. Then he thought of his children. He
had never cared for them; but to-night his
own mind seemed so soft and gentle—like to
that of "a weaned child"—that the thought of
them somehow filled his eyes with moisture. He
took a candle from the table, opened the door,
and listened. The servants were feasting, and
surmising, below stairs; Margaret was in her
own apartment. Noiselessly he made his way
to the nursery, and, entering it, laid a light kiss
on the cheek or forehead of each sleeping baby.
Then he returned to the dining-room, where,
after a moment, he loudly rang the bell. Only
too eagerly, for once in their careers, a servant
entered at either door. He despatched one of
them to summon the rest of his fellows to the
dining-room, and by the other sent a message to
Margaret, requesting her presence there also.
In a surprisingly few minutes the troop of
permanent and occasional domestics, with difficulty restraining the outward tokens of that
curiosity which they felt, had to a man filed into
the room; and Margaret, still clad in her rich
dress, was not far behind them.

The Nabob had resumed his charming, man-of-the-world demeanour of the earlier part of the evening. He jested slightly with one of the women, and politely desired that all the servants would be seated. Those of them who had known him longest afterwards declared they had never before seen their master to such advantage. Then—when Margaret, wonderingly, entered the room—with a grace of gesture that was truly courtly, he placed a chair for her, and, speaking clearly and deliberately, thus addressed his audience:

"My friends, I merely wished you to bear witness that, *by the law of Scotland, this lady is my wife.*" And then, with a wave of the hand, "I need not detain you further—go back and enjoy yourselves."

The menials flocked out of the room, and Margaret, overwhelmed by mingled surprise and gratitude, would have commenced a tearful scene with him whom, as it seemed, she had now a right to call her husband. But he lightly put her aside and left her, alleging some commonplace excuse. Thereupon she went to another room, and, in a strange flutter of feeling, sat down at her writing-desk.

During the past five years, the erring woman had not been without her own thoughts. Her father, now an old man, when first he had heard of her disgrace, had vowed never to see her face

again whilst she continued Mather's mistress.
And he had kept his word. So that she—having
with years come to think differently upon many
matters—whether firmly convinced or not of the
validity of the hasty, informal marriage, now
eagerly embraced the earliest opportunity of
informing him that the stigma on her name had
been removed, and so effecting a reconciliation.
But she had scarcely yet composed herself sufficiently to write intelligibly, when she was startled
by hearing the report of a gun ring through
the house. It was followed by a heavy fall. The
noises came from the room just overhead—that
in which Dixon kept his fire-arms. Seized with
a terror which she dared not define, Margaret
fled towards it. The servants from all directions
were already hastening thither. And, through
the crowded entry and the open door, she beheld
upon the floor the lifeless form of the man who,
but half-an-hour before, had become her husband,
—not only as he had previously been in the sight
of God, but in the eye of the law as well. He
had put a bullet through his brain. Thus did the
proud and petulant Nabob bring true his hasty
words to the Lord Lieutenant—that the day on
which he wedded Margaret should be the day of
his own death.

The question of the legitimacy of Margaret's
children was contested in the law-courts of
Edinburgh, where a verdict was given in their

favour. This not proving satisfactory to him, was appealed against by Mather's next-of-kin; and, finally, the plea was transferred to the higher tribunal. There, however, the first ruling was sustained—with the result that to this day the representative of his descendants possesses and enjoys the Nabob's estate.

"TROLLING FORTH HIS SONG."

# WILL WINTER AND ROB SCOTT.

IT is a mistake to suppose that the genuine peasant-tale is altogether a thing of the past. Certainly it is true that the old stories which introduce the supernatural and can no longer be believed have very nearly ceased to be told ; but there are other, more credible, tales which have taken their place. Such are, for instance, the stories of buried treasures—alluded to in a previous tale. Such, again, are the legends of old local battles, and of how some stream, or river, in the neighbourhood where the battle was fought ran with blood for three whole days after the fighting. Such, also, are the stories of mysterious caverns into which persons enter, but from which they do not come out. There is one cave of this kind, for instance, into which a huntsman and a pack of hounds pursued a hunted fox ; but from which neither fox, hounds, huntsman, nor horse, were ever known to emerge again. Then there is a second cave, into which a piper penetrated, playing upon his pipes. He never came out either. The music

which he made was listened to for a long time
by persons at the mouth of the cave.  At first it
was loud and cheerful, then it grew fainter and
fainter, more plaintive and more plaintive yet,
—until at last it died away in the bowels of
the earth.  Then there are kindred stories of
subterranean passages of great length—sometimes said to have been fashioned by the monks
—uniting ancient castles, or religious establish-
ments.  Then, again, there are modern varieties
of the hero-tale,—stories of fights, and of adven-
tures by flood and field.  A favourite one is that
of a prodigious leap taken by the hero in escaping
from pursuit.  There are also stories of remarkable local characters—the desperate ones being
generally preferred.  There is, for instance, the
history of the dissipated and sceptical country-
gentleman, who, having led a merry life and scoffed
at the Minister, preserved at least the virtue of con-
sistency by leaving directions in his will that he
should be buried in a vaulted chamber, seated at
a table, with a church-warden pipe in his mouth
and a bottle and a glass before him.  Or else
there is the narrative of that other reprobate,
who, when land was gone and money spent,
resolved to put an end to his life.  So he blind-
folded a favourite mare, mounted her, and rode
towards the cliff-heads.  There, he put her to
the gallop, and prepared for a leap into space.
But, just as she reached the cliff-edge, by some

instinct the blind mare swerved and turned.
The rider set her at the frightful leap again, and
again she refused ; and after a third failure,
seeing the error of his ways, he rode home, and
from that day led a reformed life.   Then, lastly,
there is the murder-tale—the story of a desperate
deed.   This must not be hastily classed with
the literature of the " penny dreadful" or the
"shilling shocker" order ; for, whatever may be
the shortcomings of Arcadia, vulgarity, at least,
is not one of them, and the peasant-tales never
sink to so low a level as that.   Blood may be
spilt in them,—and spilt freely it often is ; but
there is invariably present at least some touch
of fancy, of poetry, of character-painting, or of
the picturesque, to raise the terrible history
above the rank of the "sensation novel."   Two
examples of murder-tales, as received from the
oral tradition of the Borders, are here offered to
the reader.

The little grey village of Elsdon, in Northumberland, stands in a valley, among bare surroundings.   On passing out of it on to the Morpeth
road, the traveller finds himself lifted up on to
barren moors, where every trace of human
habitation is quickly left behind.   As he pro-
ceeds, his eye—wandering aimlessly amid the
surrounding blankness—is presently caught and
held by what seems to be an upright post ahead.
But, as he draws near it, he is astonished to

discover that the post is a gallows, from which
there dangles the hideous, black, carven effigy of
a man's head. The effect of this effigy, when
the present writer passed that way, in broad
daylight, on a March afternoon of wind and
driving cloud and rain, was by no means lacking
in eeriness. Certainly the effect of the reality
on a wayfarer passing by after dark, in a less
enlightened era, must have been little short of
appalling. "String Cross," or "Winter's Stob,"
as the gibbet is locally styled, commemorates
a murder committed in the vicinity in the late
twenties of the present century.

At that period there existed a family of
Yetholm gipsies, Winter by name, whose outrageous manners and deeds of violence had
made them hated and feared in all parts of the
Border Country to which their reputation had
penetrated. Two members of this family, a
father and son, had already suffered the extreme
penalty of the law ; and, at the time of which I
write, a second son, William, had just been set
at liberty after undergoing a term of imprisonment. William Winter was a man of a robust
bodily frame ; and he seems to have been further
endowed with a good intelligence and a strong
character. Accepting his theory of life—which
was that a man is free to prey upon society and
take his profit where he finds it,—it must be
acknowledged that he brought good gifts to the

task, or service.  For the rest, he would seem to
have been something of a ranter, and a swaggering
desperado to boot, for his traditional costume
consisted of a light-coloured coat, blue breeches,
and grey stockings ; whilst his black hair, which
he wore long, was tied in a club behind.  And,
as will be seen, he had a very good notion of
how to enjoy life, too; and—dimly perceiving,
perhaps, that his time might possibly be short—
he seems to have set himself to do so now to
the best of his ability.  One can imagine the
roving heart of the free-born " tinkler "—loathing confinement worse than death—swelling
with enthusiasm as he stood once more a free
man, outside the prison, and drew a long breath
of the free and bounteous air of heaven.  Then
he set out upon his travels.  It is rarely that a
professional vagrant travels without his " mort,"
or doxy.  Winter, a man of generous views,
associated to himself a couple of female companions.  He also obtained—no matter how, or
where—an ass, for which he had occasion ; and,
thus equipped and attended, having hatched a
little scheme, he went on his way to carry it
out.

Travelling at a leisurely rate from Newcastle,
the party arrived near Elsdon about noontide
on a summer day.  The weather was favourable; it was about dinner-time ; and, having
provisions with them, they resolved upon a

picnic. Looking round for a suitable spot,
they noticed a sheep-fold, where they would
not be likely to be disturbed. They entered
it. Winter picketed his ass, and then, seating
himself upon the ground, proceeded to cut off
pieces from a joint of mutton with his clasp-
knife, and to hand them gallantly to his fair
companions. So they feasted ; and when they
had finished, Winter's heart warming with the
good cheer, he stretched his legs before him in
the sunshine, and raised his voice and sang. One
can picture the scene : the grassy interior of
the fold, sheltered from a wind blowing without ; the ass quietly feeding at the back, and
the rollicking scoundrel trolling forth his song,
seated, like Captain MacHeath, between the
two women. What should you imagine was
the theme of his minstrelsy ? You would never
guess ; for, for a man about to commit a deed
of violence, his choice of subject was most
singular. He sang a song in praise of the
shepherd's life,—dwelling, no doubt, in amiable,
somewhat sentimental, slightly artificial, numbers
upon dewy meadows, frisking lambkins, soaring
larks, and opening flowers.

Well, what *we* imagine, *was* seen, actually
seen, and heard by an eye and ear where neither
eye nor ear were thought to be. There had
been a little herd laddie watching sheep upon
the upland that morning ; and, upon seeing the

approach of intruders of such questionable
aspect, he had withdrawn unseen, and had
hidden himself among the " bunches " of the
fold.   And there ensconced he now lay all the
time, and observed, with a child's surely and
minutely observing eye, the proceedings of the
three gipsies.  Among other things, he noted
the pattern of the clasp-knife which had been
used in cutting up the mutton, and the
arrangement of the hob-nails in Winter's shoes,
as the latter sat with his legs stretched out
before him, basking in the sun.  And, when
called upon to do so afterwards, he was able to
identify these things.

Night came, and with it Winter's season of
activity.   Not far from the sheep-fold where the
marauders had eaten and drunk—at a place
known as The Raw, situated to the north of the
Grasslees burn—lived an old woman who made
her living by travelling with a basket furnished
with articles for sale, and who was reputed
to have saved some money.  Of this money,
Winter had determined to become the possessor.
Accordingly, after nightfall, he went to the
cottage, the door of which he prized open with
a plough-coulter.   He then secured his booty;
and, this done, would have turned his back on
the premises had it not been for one of his
companions, who urged him to make short work
with the old woman, lest she should live to give

evidence against him.    Why is it that a merciless
woman is more merciless than a merciless man ?

The bloody deed accomplished, the murderer
and his associates took the road without loss of
time.    With morning, the murder was discovered.
The news that a hideous crime had been perpe-
trated in that quiet spot would doubtless spread
like wild-fire.    The neighbourhood was quickly
agog ; and, amid the endless idle clatter which
ensued, the herd laddie's story came out, and the
hue-and-cry was raised.    Winter and his companions were pursued, overtaken, and brought
back ; and, to cut a long story short, they were
convicted, mainly upon the shepherd boy's
evidence, and all three sentenced to death.    The
male ruffian was hanged in chains, and his body
was afterwards gibbeted within sight of the spot
where the crime had been committed.    There it
was allowed to remain until the bones dropped,
when they were collected in a tarred canvas bag
and hung up once more.    In time the bag de-
cayed, and in its turn fell to pieces; but even
then the popular notion of justice was not satisfied, for the gallows was still kept standing, and
a wooden figure representing the murderer was
suspended from it.    This figure may, or may not,
have been since renewed ; in any case, as I have
already said, the head is all that is left to-day.
It now only remains to add that the shepherd
boy, whose life was held to be in danger from

the vengeance of Winter's friends, was taken under the protection of a neighbouring gentleman, a magistrate, into whose service he entered. After a time, however, it was deemed expedient to remove him to a distance. A situation was, accordingly, found for him in the north of Scotland; but when he had occupied it for a short time, and whilst still a young man, he was sent home again in delicate health, where he soon afterwards died.

The scene of my second story lies across the Border. A few years before the date of Winter's murder, there resided not far from Fannsloanend, in Berwickshire, a certain Robert Scott, as peaceable, kindly, and well-disposed a working-man as you might wish to meet. Rob, who was a very simple-minded fellow, was remarkable for his powerful and athletic frame; and, as is usually the case with such men, he was a great popular favourite. Among other feats of strength and agility which he had performed, a race which he ran with the mail coach from Edinburgh to Gordon may be mentioned. The race was a close one; for Rob managed, by taking short cuts and by gaining on his rival during stoppages, to keep up with the coach all the way. Bets were thus freely indulged in by the passengers; whilst, as the hour for the arrival of the coach approached, the people of Gordon turned out in large numbers to view the finish. At that time

10

it seemed as if the runner must certainly be beaten, for the coach was just behind him and was advancing at full gallop. But, upon reaching Gordon Moss, to the surprise of every one, Scott without hesitation plunged into it; and by cleverly picking his way across upon firm ground, and by leaping a wide " stank" which intersected it, he contrived to pass the winning-post, amid the greatest enthusiasm, a few moments before the coach.

Scott had married a girl named Miller, over whose birth (as may be stated by the way) there hung a certain amount of mystery; for she was supposed to be of gentle parentage on the father's side—the offspring of an irregular alliance. They resided at a place which is known as Lightfield. They had several children, and Rob was doing well in life. His wife, in after times, declared that there was not a more harmless body than her husband extant, or one generally easier to do with. But she was obliged to add that she had known him subject to fits of ungovernable rage, during which she could do nothing with him.

Under the most favourable auspices in the world, with the lightest heart under his waistcoat, and the kindest feelings towards all men in his breast, Rob set out from home one spring morning to attend the hiring at Earlston. On his way through the crowded thoroughfares of the place, he happened to fall in with two young

men from Greenlaw, whom he knew.   Without
the smallest provocation on his part, these two
young men began to assail him with rude
banter.   Rob was touchy when provoked, yet
he managed to keep his temper ; but the two
young men, observing their advantage, persevered in their outrageous conduct, following
their victim about the hiring during the greater
part of the day, and tormenting him well-nigh
beyond human endurance.   At length Rob
shook them off; but their insults still rankled in
his breast.   There is always drink in plenty on
these occasions ; and Rob, the popular favourite,
would be sure to have his full share of work to
do in the matter of treating and "being tret."
As the liquor mounted to his head, the sense of
injury under which he smarted grew stronger,
and at last the recollection of the insults he had
received became almost intolerable.   At length,
when the hour was late, he set out to make his
way home.   The two young men had not yet
left Earlston.

The country to the east of Fannsloanend now
consists of airy spaces of pasture and tilled land,
bordered by the black woods of Mellerstain,
which in their turn are backed by the pleasant
wooded hill of Mellerstain.   In Scott's day, the
road, or track, which is known by the name of
Lightfield Entry, lay across a moor ; and there
were some small agricultural holdings, tenanted

by cottars, in the vicinity. Along this road
Scott journeyed till he reached the beginning of
the wood called Beaver's Plantation, and there
he stopped. He was still raging internally, and
he now took the stump of a young fir tree from
the fail-dyke which bounded the road, and, thus
armed, awaited his enemies. By this time it
was quite dark.

In due course, the two mischievous young
men, all unconscious of the ambush which had
been laid for them, came along the road, on their
way back to Greenlaw. As they reached the
corner of the plantation, Rob fell suddenly upon
them. Two or three blows were quickly struck,
and then there was no further resistance. The
assailant laboured under the terrible, though
paradoxical, disadvantage of excessive power.
In the heat of the moment he had not measured
his strength, and the two young men now lay
motionless on the ground before him. No
sooner did he see this, than a strong reaction set
in in Rob's simple mind. He was entirely
taken aback at the sudden collapse of his
enemies; and, horrified at what he dimly
dreaded might be the cause of it, he ran with
all speed to seek assistance. The cottage of
"Henless," where he was known, was not far off.
He tapped on the window, and the occupant, a
man named Alexander Robertson, responded to
his summons; whereupon Scott, in great agita-

tion, demanded " water, in God's name." Questioned as to the purpose for which he required it,
he at once confessed his act, at the same time
expressing his hope of resuscitating the two
men, who, he trusted, were not yet beyond the
reach of aid.    Summoning a neighbour, by name
William Watson, Robertson then returned with
Scott to the plantation, where they found one of
the young men already dead, and the other at
the last gasp.    Seeing how matters stood,
Watson urged the unhappy Scott to fly for his
life, this being all that there was now left for
him to do.    But, whether that he preferred to
face the consequences of his act, or that he was
too much broken in spirit to take any action
whatever, Scott, now entirely overcome by
remorse, declined to resort to this means of
safety.    The mangled bodies were removed to
the house of one Alexander Corsbie, in the
neighbourhood; and Scott returned to his home
and went to bed, where early next morning he
was arrested.

He was tried for his life and condemned to
be hanged, and it was arranged that the execution to take place as near as might be to
the scene of the murders.    As the day drew
near, the popular sympathy felt for Scott reached
a very high pitch.    He was well and widely
known throughout the district, where his
pleasant, unpretentious character had made him

a favourite, whilst his various feats of physical
strength had caused him to be regarded almost
in the light of a hero.   It was felt, furthermore,
that the murders had been committed in a
moment of madness, under gross provocation ;
whilst they were also in a measure accidental.
And, again, the conduct of the criminal in
declining to fly for his life brought over sympathy to his side.   However, time went on, and
no reprieve was forthcoming—the fact that Scott
had deliberately lain in wait for his victims
weighing heavily against him.   At last the fated
day arrived, and numbers of people from the
country round about travelled many miles to
view the execution.   I have not myself met with
any one who was actually present at it ; but I
am indebted to a venerable and esteemed friend
—an eye-witness of what he relates—for the
following particulars of the prisoner's journey to
the scaffold.

My friend was at that time a boy.   He had
been given a day's holiday, and had decided to
spend it, with some of his companions, in a
trout-fishing expedition.   They fished in the
Leader, down stream—baiting with salmon roe,
—and killed a large number of fish.   But, all at
once, there came a strange diversion in the midst
of their fishing.   As the boys drew near the
Leaderfoot bridge, they beheld two troops of
mounted soldiers advancing along the road,

from opposite quarters, to meet each other.
These proved to be, respectively, troops of
the Roxburghshire and of the Berwickshire
Yeomanry Cavàlry.   In the centre of the Roxburghshire troop was a carriage; and in this
carriage were seated a Minister of the Gospel,
two Officers of Justice, and the whilom popular
hero, Rob Scott, on his way from Jedburgh Jail
to the place of execution.   The face of the condemned man, as seen by my friend, was deadly
pale.   Arrived at the bridge, the Roxburghshire
guard handed over their charge to the Berwickshire men, and the two cavalcades proceeded,
each on its own way.   Rob's bearing and conduct are said to have been simple, dignified, and
manful to the last.   One trifling incident affords
a measure of the pitch to which sympathy for
him had risen.   A short time before reaching
Leaderfoot bridge, the procession had stopped
at an inn to water the horses.   Whilst this was
being done, the clergyman and the criminal
were conducted to a private room, and there left
alone together.   The room had windows which
reached almost to the ground, and the clergyman afterwards declared that, while they were
waiting there, he could not help hoping that
Scott would attempt an escape.   Once outside
the inn, his combined strength and fleetness of
foot would have stood him in good stead ; and,
with the number of friends—some of them

powerful ones—which he had in the country,
he would have had, at least, a good chance of
getting clear away.   However, no such idea
seems to have entered his head ; or, if it did,
he refrained from attempting to put it into
practice.

When, after his death, Scott's brain came to
be examined, it was found to weigh only as
much as that of an ordinary child,—and this
notwithstanding the fact that he was a big man.
It seems possible, therefore, that he was not
wholly responsible for all his actions.   At any
rate—whatever the excuses found for him—he
survives in Border tradition as a character of the
Ajax type—by no means the least sympathetic
type of hero.

A little son of his, who, in ignorance of his
father's impending fate, was herding cows near
the scene of the execution, is said to have
inquired of his grandfather what brought so
many people to the place.   Another little boy
of the time, now a very old man, has told me
that, on the day in question, he was out in a
turnip-field in a far-off part of the country, and
that he remembers seeing a relative who was
with him look at his watch, and then pronounce
the words, " It will be all over by this time."
Years afterwards, when the field in which the
execution took place was brought under the
plough, the sawn-off stumps of the scaffold poles

were discovered.    The place bears the name of
Rob Scott to this day.    And so does time heal
old wounds and sores in some natures, that I
have heard an old resident in the neighbourhood
declare that she had often in after-times seen
the widow of Scott cutting grass for her cow
within a few yards of the spot where her
husband had expiated his crime.

# THE RESURRECTIONISTS.

ECKFORD, like Hownam, has its legend of Sabbath-breakers Punished. On a slope of the hill known as Hownam Steeple, five upright stones—by some reputed a druidical circle—are vulgarly known as The Shearers and the Bandster, and are supposed to represent five harvesters who, presuming to obtrude their labours upon the holiness of the Sabbath day, were straightway turned to stone, as a judgment upon themselves and a warning to ages to come. The Eckford legend is as follows. Many years ago, there resided in the parish a certain sceptical blacksmith of an independent character. It is not said that he was anything but a quiet and hard-working man, yet his goings-on were the scandal of the neighbourhood; for, on Sunday morning, when the decent church-goers passed his shop on their way to attend public worship, they would behold him at his work as usual. It was then felt, naturally enough, that the man who boldly pursued his labours seven days a week took a mean advantage of his neighbours,—an advantage which to keen competitors in the race of life (and where are there competitors so keen as among our sturdy Borderers?) must have been particularly galling. True it was always open to them to fall back on the comforting reflection that, though the present moment was the blacksmith's, the remote and vague future was theirs. Then—as they would, doubtless, eagerly assure themselves—it must go hardly with him. Yet this reflection was not wholly satisfactory either; for, whatever might be the awful pains and penalties which they would have the happiness of seeing neighbour Burn-the-Wind endure in another world, the fact remained that for them the present moment had a force and pertinacity of appeal which nothing else in the world could match. In other words, the bird in the hand was the bird which they instinctively in their secret hearts preferred. In these circumstances, lest bad example should corrupt good manners, Providence—as was its way in the good old times—stept in (perhaps it was none too soon), with the following result. On a certain Sabbath morning, as they passed the smithy as usual, the church-goers beheld their neighbour as usual at his work. But, a few hours later, when they returned from church, neither the blacksmith, nor his wife, nor his family, nor his smithy, nor yet a vestige of any one of them was to be seen. The place where

the blacksmith's shop had stood—near the
south-west corner of the field to the west of the
manse—was now a bog! And so doubly
accursed, through the misdeeds of its former
occupant, had it become, that a belief soon prevailed in the neighbourhood that this bog could
never be drained. And so, for many years, it
actually remained undrained. At length, the
curse being removed, the draining was accomplished. But—as if to confirm the tradition,
or to act as a last caution to the parishioners—
in the course of the draining operations a smith's
anvil was brought to light. The hill at the foot
of which the bog was situated, is still—or was
till lately—known as The Smithy Hill; whilst
of the people of Eckford it may be said that
they remain exemplary, or, at least, typical,
churchmen to this day.

Their little quaint old-fashioned kirk and its
kirkyard possess two or three features of
interest. Beside the church-door, for example,
hangs an iron collar, or "jougs," used in former
days for the punishment of those who came
under church discipline. The author of the
Wilkie Manuscript informs us that, about the
middle of the last century, such characters were
condemned to stand three days at the kirk-door
in the jougs, clothed in a sackcloth gown called
"the sacking gown." After occupying this
position of public ignominy, they were con-

ducted by the betheral to the well-known "stool of repentance," where they sat till the sermon was finished, when they were duly admonished— "clapper-clawed" is the irreverent young doctor's term—by the Minister. Then they would be removed outside once more, and replaced in the jougs until the congregation had left the church.

The jougs were fastened round the offender's neck by means of a staple and padlock, and there is a story connected with their discontinuance at Eckford. It is said that the last person upon whom they were used, being of unusually short stature, had to be raised upon a stone to reach the necessary elevation. During the earlier part of the church service, the stone happened to slip from under the culprit's feet, and when in due course the church-officer went out to bring in his prisoner, it was found that he (or she) had been hanged by the neck till he was dead. After this occurrence, the jougs were used no more. It is not with the jougs, however, but with a small castellated tower, or look-out, which occupies one corner of the churchyard, that our present narrative is concerned.

The intense excitement spread through the country by the discovery of the Tanner's Close, or West Port, murders, in the year '28, gave place to another scare which was scarcely less appalling. The execution of the murderer Burke might allay such fears as were entertained on behalf of the living ; but, as people now knew, they had reason to fear for their dead as well. The evidence at the trial had attracted public attention to the existence of a hideous commerce in the country.  This commerce dealt with a merchandise no less ghastly than the products of the charnel-house themselves ; and, whatever the horrors of the trade, it was felt that the largeness of the gains which it realised —as much as sixteen pounds being known to have been given for a body—would always ensure a sufficient number of persons ready to engage in it.  Stories of rifled graves—doubtless duly multiplied and exaggerated—were passed eagerly from mouth to mouth, until at last a panic fear possessed the multitude, so that the very acme of wretchedness—an empty hyperbole of language as it had always hitherto been accounted—seemed in actual fact to have been realised, for the dead no longer rested in their graves.

At the time when this scare was at its height, a certain young packman, James Goodfellow by name, was one night passing along the road which lies between Jedburgh and Kelso.  The season was the late autumn, when nights are long ; and the moon, which was in her last quarter, had not yet risen.  It was very dark, and the hour was very late ; for James Goodfellow— or "Dandy Jim," as he was more commonly called—had been visiting a sweetheart in the neighbourhood, and their interview had been tender and prolonged. Now, at the time I speak of, even to be abroad, alone, and at such an hour, taxed the nerve; for fiction had reinforced the horrors of fact, and legends of nocturnal perils awful and mysterious abounded. To name a single instance, a belated rustic had told how, as he lay in the ditch where his potations had deposited him, he had beheld as it were the phantom of a dog-cart pass him, driven by an austere and cruel-looking man wearing black. What gave its phantasmal character to the equipage was the absolute soundlessness of its movement—the wheels of the cart and the horse's shoes being evidently, for some suspicious purpose or other, sheathed in india-rubber. Hidden in the ditch, the toper saw and was himself unseen; but (if what he afterwards averred were true) he had a narrow escape with his life, for he declared that the driver of the dog-cart carried a scythe, and that, perambulating the solitary thorough-fares after dark, his practice was to steal up noiselessly behind the unsuspecting wayfarer, to mow him down, and transmit his body by some secret agency to the surgeons of Edinburgh.

Dandy Jim, however, who was a stout fellow, considered that the attractions of an interview with his sweetheart more than overbalanced the dangers of the road. He was not easily frightened; and he was, furthermore, superior in manner and intelligence to the general run of the class to which he belonged, whilst his experience as a packman had given him a knowledge of the world and a readiness of resource in difficulties to which the ordinary peasant cannot pretend. He was reputed to have been successful in business and to have saved money, and was in fact on the point of marriage with the sweetheart above alluded to.    But this is by the way.

Proceeding on his road, as he drew near Eckford, Jim was puzzled to observe a pale, luminous haze—like a mist above water—which seemed to rise from the churchyard.  He could not understand it; for, though he remembered that a burial had taken place there on the previous day, he was of a somewhat sceptical turn of mind, and rejected the idea of a corpse-candle. Neither—though his head was full of stories of body-snatchers—could he quite bring himself to believe in the actuality of all that he had heard. The surrounding country (so far, at least, as he knew) had hitherto escaped the depredations of the resurrectionists; and it somehow seemed to him in the last degree unlikely that those foul and fantastic plunderers of whom he had lately heard so much should pursue their unholy avocations in the remote and quiet graveyard of Eckford.   Had he given a second thought to the matter, he must have recognised the fact that

the very remoteness and quietness of the spot
marked it out as especially suitable for their
purpose.

In the meantime the puzzling light had
disappeared. "An optical illusion," thought the
Dandy, and strode onward on his way. But, no!
For there was the luminous haze once more.
And it was brighter than any autumnal mist
could be, even leaving out of consideration the
fact that to-night there was neither moon nor
star in heaven from which light could be
drawn. Dandy Jim was perplexed; but not
alarmed. Under cover of the darkness, he stept
forward noiselessly, and leaning his arms upon
the churchyard wall, peered before him and
endeavoured to reconnoitre. By this time the
ghostly light had again disappeared, and he could
see nothing. But he could hear; and, from the
place where the light had been, there now came
a sound. It was like the sound of tearing, or
rending. Jim listened, and for a moment his
heart stood still. Then, there seemed to be a
quick movement at the place from which the
sound had proceeded, and all at once a startling
flood of light gushed forth. Upon this light, as
on a background, appeared the gigantic black
shadow of a man. In another instant the shadow
had passed into the surrounding night, and the
light had disappeared. Then there was heard a
stifled oath, followed by a murmured expostu-

11

lation. Jim understood exactly what had happened. There were evidently persons work- ing in the churchyard by the light of a dark lantern. Through some clumsiness of theirs, the slide of the lantern had slipt back, whereupon the imprisoned light had gushed forth, bearing upon it, as upon a flood, the shadow of a man occupy- ing a position between the light and the onlooker.

Ninety-nine out of every hundred rustics of those days, when they had seen so much, would probably have taken to their heels—and small blame to them if they did. But Jim, as has been stated, was no common countryman. His quick eye, during the momentary illumination, had taken in more than has been described, and he had by this time fully grasped the situation. On the further side of the gigantic shadow—whose back was turned towards him—he had discerned a yawning pit; and he now realised that his first supposition had been wrong, and that—likely or unlikely—there were actually resurrectionists at their ghoulish work in the quiet graveyard before him.

As soon as he felt certain of this fact, Jim's courage rose to the occasion, and his first thought was how to circumvent the sacrilegious mid- night thieves. The spot was solitary. The quiet agricultural population had long since betaken themselves to their beds ; and to seek assistance now would, as he saw, be merely to

waste the precious time, and to give the in-
human depredators a good chance of getting
safely away with their ghastly booty. No; Jim
felt that he must tackle them alone; and as, for
aught he knew to the contrary, they might be
numerous; he also recognised that it must be
by cunning rather than by force. But he felt
himself equal to the task.

Having removed his boots, and deposited
them where he would be able to find them again,
the packman now set out upon a noiseless tour
of discovery round the outside of the wall which
enclosed the churchyard. For some time his
search was unrewarded; but, presently, after
entering the Minister's paddock, his strained
sense of hearing was met by a slight sound
which he had been expecting to hear. It was
that of a horse cropping grass. He continued
to grope his way along the wall, and a black
body, just perceptible in the darkness, soon rose
in front of him. Subjected to the touch, this
body proved to represent a horse and gig. The
horse was tethered to one of the churchyard
trees, and had evidently been withdrawn, with
the gig, to this side field, in order to be screened
from observation from the road. After some
trouble, the Dandy loosed the tether, and then,
kicking the animal smartly in the ribs, sent him
off at a frightened gallop, dragging the gig
behind him over the uneven surface of the field.

The thud of the horse's hoofs and the jolting of
the vehicle at once disturbed the body-snatchers
at their work.   They were but two in number,
and both of them new to the job and somewhat
nervous ; so that, realising that their one means
of escape in case of a surprise was slipping
through their hands, they at once sprang to
their feet, and with smothered imprecations and
ejaculations of anxiety set off in pursuit of the
runaway beast.   This was exactly what Jim had
intended that they should do.   He now bent
down, so as to be covered by the wall, and running along beside it in a direction contrary to
that taken by the horse, began presently to neigh.

" This  way ! "  muttered one of the robbers
to the other under his breath ; and, stumbling
over graves and breaking their shins against
headstones in their haste, they set off upon the
false scent.   Jim neighed once more—this time
at a point still further remote from the true
one ; and then, when the interrupted resurrectionists had scrambled over the wall out of the
churchyard in pursuit of their runaway, he
scrambled into it.   By this time the rising
moon had begun to shed her radiance above
the horizon, and a faint light overspread the
landscape.

When he had made his way towards the spot
to which his eye had first been attracted by the
lantern-light, a ghastly sight met the packman's

gaze. At his feet lay an open grave, the contents
of which had been abstracted. Beside it, on the
trodden earth, lay the coffin, which had been
clumsily prized open—the lid having been
broken in the process. The leaden inner shell,
thus exposed to view, had also been ripped up.
It was empty. Glancing about, in the half-
light, Jim's eye now fell upon an oblong pack-
age, enveloped in a black cloth. He stooped
and lifted a corner of the cloth, and his
suspicions were at once proved true. To
remove the black pall from the body, to raise
the latter in his arms and to conceal it behind a
neighbouring grave, were for the packman the
work of a moment. This done, he returned to
the grave-side, and having carefully enveloped
himself from head to foot in the black pall or
cloth, proceeded to lie down at full length in the
exact place where a moment before the exhumed
corpse had lain. Then for a time all was silence
and stillness as of death. By-and-by there was
a sound of advancing footsteps, and the body-
snatchers returned. They seemed flurried and
out of breath, and one of them was cursing
horribly.

"Didn't I tell you that it was as much as
our lives were worth if she should chance to
break loose?" said he, in a harsh voice, in the
interval between two volleys of imprecations.

"Sure the beast must be human, I believe,

to lowze the knot tied!" replied a second
speaker, who spoke with the accent of one
who is accustomed to be ordered about and
to be taken to task, yet who seeks to conciliate
his tyrant.

During this time Jim, whose head was closely
covered, could of course see nothing; but he
gathered from the footsteps and the voices that
there were not more than two body-snatchers
present, which greatly reassured him. What
puzzled him much was that he half fancied he
recognised their voices. The first speaker now
swore a few more terrifying oaths and gave
vent to some more denunciations. "If ever I
come out again on sic an eerand wi' the likes
o' you," he wound up, "I desairve to be transported!"

The owner of the smaller voice, who—
whether from native impotency or accidental
circumstance—seemed to enjoy no freedom of
speech or action whatsoever, confined himself
to murmuring something deprecating in reply.
But his humility only served further to incense
his bullying associate, who now desired him,
in tones of fresh irritation, not to stand talking
there all night, but to "bear a hand."

"We've put off owre muckle time a'ready.
Damme! See, yonder's the mune. Well, if
we both of us swing for this job before Jethart
jail, it's none o' my wyte, mind you that!"

As these words were uttered, Jim felt himself grasped by the head and feet, and raised from the ground. As best he could, he simulated a dead weight.

" My ! " exclaimed the second of the speakers, with a puff of exhaustion, " but the corp is a heavy one, Hare."

The other gruffly enjoined silence.

Now, on hearing the more desperate of the two body-snatchers addressed by the name of Hare, the pretended corpse had very nearly betrayed his animation by starting. It was not that he feared to find himself in the power of the murderer of the same name—the dramatic story of whose exit from Scotland he had heard, —but that the pronouncing of the vocable at once cleared up the mystery which had previously puzzled him as to the identity of the miscreants in whose hands he had chosen to place himself. In his capacity as a packman, his acquaintance was numerous, and extended over a wide tract of country ; and it now flashed across his mind that the voices which he had from the first seemed to recognise were those of two drunken journeymen tailors, or " Whip-the-cats," of Greenlaw, generally known to their associates by the by-names of The Rabbit and The Hare. In fact, the only thing which had prevented Dandy Jim from making the recognition at the first was the

unaccustomed tone of firmness and authority
assumed on this occasion by the Hare,—a
veritable ninth part of a man, who had been
hitherto known to him as much for his unctuous
and cringing demeanour as for the dishonest
shiftiness of his character.   In person the Hare
was a tall, lean figure, whose cadaverous countenance well fitted him for his part of lycan-
thropist.   The Rabbit, on the other hand,
was short and round-about in figure, with grog-
blossoms about his nose, and a falling chin and
open mouth.   Once he knew into whose hands
he had fallen, Jim vowed that the drunken
scoundrels should pay dearly for their exploit.

During all this time, he was being borne
unsteadily along in the direction of the gig,—
into which, after several unsuccessful efforts on
the part of his bearers, he at last found himself
hoisted.   Meanwhile, the nervous trepidation
of the body-snatchers seemed momentarily to
increase ; and after a brief whispered consul-
tation, it was decided between them that there
was no time to return to the grave to efface the
traces of their theft.   They, therefore, without
further delay, led the horse and gig back to the
road, took their places one on either side of the
supposed dead body, whipt up, and drove away.
The packman's object was now to discover from
their conversation the names of the accomplices
by whose aid they were to dispose of their

unnatural plunder. Their possession of the horse and gig, as well as the daring nature of the adventure—so foreign upon this account, though on no other, to the character of the persons engaged—made him also suspect that the tailors were the tools of other parties behind them; whilst the fact, which soon made itself apparent, that they were both under the influence of liquor, indicated that they had been primed for the job.

Having taken the road leading towards Kelso, the occupants of the gig drove on for some time almost without speaking. Entirely enveloped in his sable covering, Jim had stiffened himself out, with his feet against the foot-board of the vehicle, like a dead body in a state of rigour, which position he with some trouble maintained. But he soon discovered that a gradual change was taking place in the frame of mind of his companions. Whether because the effect of the liquor which they had imbibed was wearing off, or because—the necessity of action being over—their nerves had collapsed, it was evident that a feeling of uneasiness arising from the proximity of the corpse was stealing over them.

Meantime, having passed the park-fence of Sunlaws, they had reached the village of Heiton. It was sunk in deep slumber. They passed through it and drove on. By this time the melancholy, wasted moon had risen above the horizon, and it now faintly illumined the wide surrounding landscape, which was still and silent to the point of awe. To their left, the Eildon Hills, Peniel Heugh, Down Law, Smailholm Tower, and Sweethope and Mellerstain Hills, indented the sky-line. To the right, wild, un-enclosed, moorland country rose above Ladyrig toward the blackness of Bowmont Forest. For some time past the poor Rabbit's spirits had been sinking ever lower and lower. And now, at last,—though he knew that by breaking the silence he would incur the dreaded wrath of his companion,—he felt that, at any cost, he must be comforted by the sound of a human voice, and that a courageous one. So, after several attempts which died upon his lips, he at length, in quavering tones, made an obser-vation. The result was even worse than he had expected. It is true that there was no anger in the voice of the Hare, as he spoke in reply; but there was that which was worse to listen to than any anger. His accent had weirdly changed from that of half-an-hour before, and the stifled tones to which he now gave utterance were alone enough to make a man's flesh creep and the hair rise on his scalp. They were those of a man who sweats with fear. Now, among weaklings, there is nothing in the world so contagious as terror; and thus when the Rabbit became aware that the condition of his companion—upon whom until now he had relied—was worse than his own, he felt that his fears had not yet done justice to the awfulness of the occasion, and thereupon his teeth positively chattered. The packman, beneath his coverlet, heard the sound, and chuckled to himself.

Meantime, to the infected fancy of the frightened men, the horse seemed to advance at a snail's pace, as though it wore invisible shackles. The road was as unfrequented as the wilderness, and the moonlit landscape seemed to wear an eerie and unearthly aspect.

" I would give ten years of my life for a dram," gasped with dry lips the Hare.

" You'll get it at the shebeen at the Broadloan Toll," replied his mate ; " but that's far off—unco far off—yet."

This was cold comfort.

The night was close, and by this time Dandy Jim had begun to grow uncomfortably warm beneath his coverings. Neither had he now any reason for remaining where he was, for a remark dropped by the Rabbit had revealed to him that the destination of the body-snatchers was Greenlaw, and that a carrier plying between that town and Edinburgh was the agent upon whom they depended for the transmission of the body. This was all he had wanted to know, and he now waited only for an effective opportunity to declare himself. The farms of Heiton East Mains,

Maisondieu, and Wallace's Nick were by this
time passed, and the village of Maxwellheugh
was nearly reached.   At last the Rabbit, whose
condition, for some reason or other, had for
some time past been growing more and more
acutely distressing, could bear it in silence no
longer, but broke out wildly :

"Hare! I'll take an oath before a Justice of
the Peace I felt the body stir!"

But the Hare's distress was even more extreme
than that of his associate.

"Rabbit, man!   Rabbit, man!" murmured
he, in the hushed and solemn tones of dire
mental tribulation, "my mind misgives me, my
mind misgives me, but we hae mistaken our
man.   They must ha' buried this one alive, I'm
thinking ; for, as I'm a living sinner, *the corp is
warm !*"

This was the moment for which Jim had
patiently waited.   He now slowly lifted the cloth
which was about his face, and spoke, in such
sepulchral tones as he was able to command :

"*Warm*, do you say ?   And, pray, what would
you be, Mr. Hare, if ye came frae where I hae
been ?"

The Hare saw the supposed dead body move.
To his heated imagination, its action as it
uncovered its face bore a hideous resemblance
to that of a dead man rising from the grave at
the last day.   He heard the sepulchral tones

which addressed to him by name a pertinent
and suggestive query; and he waited for no
more. With a bound, like Jack-in-the-Box, he
leapt from the gig, cleared the fence which
bounded the road upon his side, and a moment
afterwards was racing for his life across the open
ground of Spylaw. At the same instant, the
Rabbit on his side slid to the ground, scrambled
through the hedge, and made for the covert of
the High Wood of Springwood Park as fast as
his short legs would carry him. Dandy Jim,
released from his cerements, clapped his hand
upon his side, and loud and long was his laughter
as he watched the two grotesque figures disap-
pearing across country in the moonlight. When
he had had his laugh out, he turned his horse's
head to the right-about, and drove briskly home
to his lodging.

The knowledge which he had gleaned from
the broken talk of the journeymen tailors led to
the timely discovery of an organised conspiracy
to snatch bodies from country grave-yards,—
which was found to be presided over by a disso-
lute publican, in conjunction with a neighbouring
farmer. The publican was thereupon compelled
to leave the country; whilst it was only with
great difficulty that the farmer's share in the
disgraceful business was, with indifferent success,
hushed up. Dandy Jim, on the other hand,
obtained considerable credit for his conduct in

the affair ; whilst, as the horse and gig were never claimed, they remained in his hands,—so that when, shortly afterwards, his sweetheart became his bride, he was able to drive her in a conveyance of his own from Eckford Kirk to the home which he had prepared for her.

It only remains to add that after this the parishioners of Eckford, prudently resolving to avoid all risks of similar outrages in the future, erected in the churchyard the little watch-tower, or look-out, which was mentioned in the commencement of this story.

Here, for a certain period after a burial had taken place, the male rate-payers of the parish nightly took it in turn to go on duty; and a respected friend of the writer has informed him that she can remember the circumstances of her father paying a man to take his turn of watching. She added that, for further security, a light would be placed upon the new-made grave. A year or two after these events, however, an Act was passed through Parliament which had for its object to legalise and regulate the supply of human bodies to the dissecting-rooms,—from which time forth the body-snatcher has found his occupation gone, and the bodies of the dead have been allowed to repose undisturbed in their graves.

# THE BROKEN TRYST.

AMONG the pastoral districts composing the
southern portion of Teviotdale, there is probably none more beautiful than that which is
known, in the common local speech, as Bowmont Water. Green and solitary, this valley
wears—at least in summer and in spring—a
soft and winning beauty, which by no means
belongs to the harsher, railroad-traversed
Liddesdale, though it is to be found again,
in the same unspoiled and primitive perfection, in certain valleys of The Forest. For
miles the softly-rounded, carelessly-moulded
Cheviot Hills stretch away uninterrupted ; and
there is less of human life in this hill world
to-day than there was a hundred years ago,—
when the main road for pack-horses over the
Border lay across Cocklaw (where now only a
track, in many places obliterated, remains);
and when a row of houses extended for some
distance down the river-bank from near the
farm of Belford. To-day no shop is to be
found nearer than Town Yethom—five miles

off; but an old lady who died only two or three years ago has spoken to the present writer of going, as a child, to spend her weekly penny on "sweeties" sold at one of the houses in this row. These dwellings of the living are now all swept away: the "narrow cells," the present abode of the former tenants of the houses, alone remain. At Mowhaugh, across the river, on the narrow flat between the water and the hills, is a small unkept, uneven, enclosure, where the grass grows green above the heads of the departed. The grave-stones still occupy their old places; but most of the flat ones among them have been tilted off the level, most of the erect have fallen from the perpendicular. And the hand of Time— who bears in mind, perhaps, that our rest is still imperfect whilst our names are yet bandied on men's lips, still imperfect until we shall be, not only dead and buried, but forgotten,—the hand of Time has passed gently over the inscriptions, obliterating them almost as completely as a school-child obliterates the ciphering on a slate. For it is only once a day, at the hour when the concentrated rays of the setting sun strike level on the lettering, that the names and ages, the births and deaths, of the forgotten dwellers in this valley become once more for a few moments to the pious eye recoverable. Yet the latest interment in this forsaken churchyard took place no longer ago than in the year 1836.

The farm of Belford was brought into the writer's family by his paternal grandmother ; but even the present farm-house, as he inclines to believe, dates from a considerably earlier period. An older house is still standing, within a short distance of the new one: it is now used as a stable, and, partly owing to its dilapidations, appears very old indeed. It has a fine, defective, old thatched roof, and " corby steps " ; and its harled walls are muffled and enveloped in the foliage—deep and dark as night and slumber— of a tree-like ivy-plant. This old house, I have been told, possessed a secret room. It was contrived beneath a landing, half-way up the staircase, and entered by a trap-door, over which a narrow stair-carpet was laid so as to conceal it. In this lair, a member of the Scott family, who had rendered himself obnoxious to the reigning powers by the part which he had taken in the Jacobite Risings of the last century, repeatedly sought refuge ; and it is said that, though the house was repeatedly searched for him, he thus escaped discovery.

At Belford, some five or six years ago, I took up my abode for a few weeks. On the evening of my arrival, going out into the green enclosure before the house, I felt delighted with my new residence. The month was April, the sky was blue, and the weather mild and lovely. All around me were grassy hills, which—though a snow-wreath might yet linger here and there in their recesses—would soon, I hoped, be at their best and greenest. And, turn where I might, I was never out of earshot of the near trickle or the distant roar of flowing water—fresh sounds, soothing, pensive, dream-compelling. Before me, within the enclosure, there was a grove of elm-trees—trees of any kind in this hill district are a rarity—in the upper branches of which the rooks were calling, among their thickly-crowded nests. These rooks, as I knew, had been carefully preserved by the late occupant of the house—a man of taste, who wished, no doubt, where human life was so scarce, to make the most of such animal life as existed. Then, as I strolled, a newly-dropt lamb came bounding up to me—mistaking me, doubtless, for the shepherd who was rearing it by hand—grasped my walking-stick between its jaws in a friendly manner, and supported itself by setting its fore feet against my leg whilst I patted and stroked it. Involuntarily I thought of the Childhood of the World. It seemed as though the Golden Age still lingered here, or were returned again. My object in coming alone into these solitudes was to study and to write, and I then and there made up my mind that my writing should take the character of the Pastoral. The surroundings would inspire nothing else—to attempt to indite a tragedy here, where the thing itself was

unknown, would be to strike a needless discord.
So I that night resolved. But Circumstance
ruled it otherwise. The experience of a few
days sufficed to change my mood, teaching me
that Sorrow, Sin, and Passion, are no strangers
to primitive life, and that the "trail of the
serpent," detected in Eden, is found also in
Arcadia. For one thing, cases of insanity
seemed numerous in proportion to the sparse-
ness of the population—healthy in mind as in
body, as one would have hoped them to be.
Instances of suicide, too, were on record.
Furthermore, this primitive world of hills had
a type of tragedy peculiar to itself,—a tragedy
in which Nature and the elements themselves
represented the dæmonic force, inspiring terror ;
whilst the shepherds, the principal inhabitants,
as protagonists, excited compassion by their
struggles and their sufferings. An instance of a
sad tragedy of this kind, which had happened
not long before, was narrated to me by an old
shepherd on the farm.

One winter's evening, when the snow lay on
the ground, Henry H——, a young shepherd, set
out to travel across the hills to the distant farm
of Blindburn. He had with him a young sheep-
dog, led by a string. Now, to the stranger, the
wild and pathless world of hills presents at
every step the danger of losing the way. Even
in daylight and when landmarks are in view,

a fog may come on at any moment, and then he is left to steer his course by the wind, which may fall or change its direction. But the shepherd, native of the wild, is generally perfectly at home there, and has no more difficulty in finding the way—however hard it may appear to another—than has a fisherman upon a sea he knows. Atmospheric conditions have, however, to be reckoned with, and these are apt to be treacherous. Henry H—— was not expected at Blindburn, and thus no notice was taken of his not arriving there at the due time. Some days later, however, some people from a house where he had rested on his journey chanced to fall in with the Blindburn people, when they casually inquired how Henry had got home that night. To their consternation, it was replied that he had never got home yet. It was felt at once that he must have perished among the hills ; however, there was nothing for it but to wait until the snow should disappear,—which did not happen for some weeks. Then the men of the neighbourhood met together to search for the missing man. His body was discovered within a stone's-throw of the place where they had agreed to assemble,—at the foot of a heugh about eight feet in height, over which in his bewilderment he had fallen. It lay upon its face. One leg was bent over the edge of a syke, or channel, and the level to which the water in the channel had reached was marked upon the dead man's breeches. I ought to have mentioned that the young dog which poor Henry had with him had returned to his home on the day following his master's departure. The string by which the dog had been led was now discovered to have been cut, and the end of it to have been thrust into the pocket of the unfortunate sufferer. This circumstance gave rise to a debate (of course impossible to determine) as to whether the shepherd had cut the string before or after his fall,—believing that the dog would follow of its own accord ; or, out of compassion, or as a forlorn hope, in order that it might run home. The story which next follows was obtained, in the course of one of my rambles, from a woman who acted as housekeeper to an old widower shepherd at the lonely cottage of Seefew, situated upon the limit of my hill-farm.

Ellen ——, was in her day the prettiest girl of those parts. Though only a shepherd's daughter, she had been sought in marriage not alone by a number of young men who were her equals in station, but by a wealthy farmer of the district as well. But, besides being a beauty, Ellen was a coquette—at least she had got a name in the neighbourhood for playing fast and loose with her admirers. Perhaps her head was a little turned. Perhaps it was only that, delighting in conquest and admiration,

and also loving novelty, she loved her liberty
more dearly than all—a collocation of tastes
which, from a woman's point of view, is surely
not an unnatural one.  And yet it had sufficed
to cause many a heartache, and to send away
many a swain from her father's door "a sadder
and a wiser man."

At last, however, it seemed as if Miss Ellen
had met her match.  And it was pronounced
by the envious to be of a piece with her general
perversity that that match was certainly the
least desirable of all which had offered.  This
is how the matter came about.  It was the
custom of the shepherds—especially of such
as were, like Ellen's father, "up in years"—
to engage additional assistance against the press
of work at lambing-time.  In this manner it
chanced that a man of the name of Fox, who was
a perfect stranger in the district, became for a
time an inmate of Ellen's father's cottage.  Fox
was not a young man.  In manner he was
moody and taciturn.  No one knew precisely
whence he came; nor did he, throughout his
sojourn in the neighbourhood, volunteer any
information upon this or kindred points.  In
a word, he kept himself to himself.  And, by
this and other means, he got himself disliked
by his fellow-workmen.  But—whether the
mystery which hung about him attracted her;
whether she was put upon her mettle by the

apparent difficulty of the conquest; or whether (as one would perhaps prefer to believe) her woman's heart was touched by the loneliness and repressed nature of the stranger—from the first it was clear that Ellen did not share the general dislike. To the jealous indignation of older admirers, she was repeatedly observed, in the course of the day's work, to select him as the recipient of trifling, yet coveted, favours. And, in short, with time it became apparent that there was an understanding betwixt them. At last the lambing-season came to an end, and with it Fox's term of residence under the same roof with Ellen. He did not, however, leave the neighbourhood ; but, being a good workman, contrived to find further temporary employment where he would not be entirely out of reach. And it was whispered by the gossips —for there is tattle even in Arcadia—that Ellen continued to meet him secretly.

The gossips were, in this instance, well-informed. In the face of her father's strong disapproval of the attachment, Ellen continued, throughout the summer, to carry on a secret correspondence with her newest admirer. And she met him whenever a meeting could be arranged ; which, however, owing to the distance at which her lover now dwelt, and to her father's vigilance, was not often.

Well, the summer passed away, and a certain

night in the early autumn arrived. Now it happened that Fox had given his sweetheart a tryst for that night, and that he had done so in a very unusual manner. For in addition to naming the place and the hour, he had made it a provision that she was not to arrive on the ground *before* the time fixed. It struck Ellen when she thought of it that this was rather a curious proviso to be made by a lover upon a like occasion ; but, notwithstanding that Fox had charged her repeatedly and impressively, she did not scruple, when the time came, to disobey his injunctions. To successfully deceive her parent was with her the prime consideration ; and, as matters chanced, the hour of her arrival at the rendezvous happened to be a good deal earlier than that which Fox had fixed for it.

The meeting-place agreed upon was a little wood situated in a glen, between two hill-sides, through which flowed a stream. The trees composing the wood were chiefly old alders ; and the place was known as the haunt of herons, who had their nests in the topmost branches of the trees. In this place, Ellen took up her station, beneath the appointed tree, and proceeded to await her lover's coming. But either he tarried long, or time seemed to pass very slowly in the solitude and darkness of the wood. At first she grew impatient, and then she grew afraid. A whimsical idea now occurred to her. It was that if she were to climb into the branches of the tree under which she stood her position would be one of greater safety and comfort. She was active; the tree was not difficult to climb; and a few minutes later she sat among its upper branches. There, among the herons' nests, she continued her watch; and at last her patience was rewarded. By the light of the moon, she beheld at some distance the figure of a man slowly wending his way up the glen. The eyes of true love—ay, and possibly even of mock love as well—are pro-verbially sharp; and the light shed by the moon sufficed for her to recognise him for whom she waited. She was on the point of descending from her coign of vantage, when she fancied that she detected an unexpected peculiarity in her lover's gait and carriage which puzzled her. As he came nearer, she found that she had not been deceived. Fox was carrying over his shoulder some heavy article, which the moon-light, catching upon its polished blade, at last revealed to be a spade. Ellen was naturally a little surprised at her lover's bringing a spade with him to their meeting in that out-of-the-way place; and, curiosity getting the better of her first impulse, she decided for the present to remain where she was and to watch his move-ments.

Arrived at the foot of the tree, Fox stood still
and looked about him. Then, after having as it
seemed made sure that his sweetheart was not
yet in sight,—for, of course, it did not occur to
him to look into the boughs overhead,—he set
to work to dig. Ellen watched his proceedings
from above. Strange stories of buried secrets
flocked into her mind, and she became breathlessly interested. Then, suddenly, Fox's repeated
injunctions to her on no account to come to the
meeting-place before the hour which he had
named flashed across her recollection. She had
no means of calculating time; but in all likelihood that hour had not yet arrived;—in which
case it was plain that her lover's present acts
were intended to be concealed from her knowledge. Her curiosity became more acute, and a
degree of awe mingled with it. For she had
never entirely divested herself of a certain
fear with which Fox had from the first inspired
her.

Meantime the digging proceeded apace, for
the ground was soft and peaty, and the delver
laboured hurriedly—furtively glancing around
him every minute or two the while. The hole
he was at work upon was not a pit; it had the
form of a trench rather. At last he paused,
rested upon the handle of his spade, and wiped
the sweat from his brow. Ellen's eyes were
riveted upon him; and, as it dawned on her

that she looked upon his finished work, a thrill
shot through her heart. It was a grave!

For whom was it intended? Alas! she dared
not answer that question. Every circumstance
seemed to point to one only possible solution
of the mystery; but the mere thought of that
solution overpowered her. That her lover should
have decoyed her treacherously to this lonely
spot to murder her seemed beyond belief. Yet,
if it was beyond belief, why did she shake with a
convulsive terror in every limb? Her trembling
shook the branches of the tree, and the leaves
rustled as if stirred by the wind. This slight
sound brought her to herself again. Collecting
her scattered faculties, she perceived clearly that
she had but one frail chance for her life :—to
remain absolutely motionless, noiseless, where
she was ; and so, through the chance of Fox's
not looking up into the tree, escape his observation. The chance was a slender one ; but as a
drowning man will catch at a straw, she caught
at it, and from that moment moved not a muscle
and scarce drew a breath.

Fox had seated himself at the foot of the tree,
with his back against it, and was, no doubt,
looking out for her coming. The moon shone
brightly; all around was still ; and there seemed
no earthly reason why, at any moment, his
glance should not be directed upward just as
well as in any other direction. Ellen realised

her danger to the full.    But, with an effort of
the will, she resolutely shut out the heart-
quelling visions which her imagination would
have thrust before her, and compelled herself
to adhere to the course of action in which, as
we have seen, her one chance of safety seemed
to lie.    The nights at this season of the year
(so she told herself in her endeavours to
fortify her mind) were not long.    Some hours
—surely, surely, some hours of the darkness
must, by this time, be already past.    With the
peep of day, the shepherds would be abroad
upon the hills again, cheerily shouting to their
dogs, and driving the sheep from their night
resorts on the hill-tops to feed in the valleys.
So, as a dying man might fix his thoughts on
heaven, did she endeavour to fix her thoughts
on the return of daylight.    And in this, the
hour of her deadly peril, fickle fortune smiled
upon the girl.    The black and shaggy head
below her was bent downwards, the eyes seemed
fixed upon the earth, as if their owner had sunk,
and was sinking every moment deeper and
deeper, into some insidious and engrossing
reverie.    So, for Ellen, racked in body, and a
prey to the most ghastly fears, the minutes
crept by with a leaden foot, every one of them
seeming to bring with it the weight of years.
    At last the moon, completing her long voyage
through the skies, drew near her haven, sank

with diminishing light towards the hill, and set
behind it. Ellen was, by this time, reduced to
a state which, miserable as it was, was yet
almost free from pain. Her mind was growing
dulled, and took little or no note of external
things; whilst she maintained her position in the
tree—already maintained, as it seemed to her,
for a lifetime—without conscious effort. The
darkness of the hour before dawn fell upon the
world. And then, from the foot of the tree
there burst forth a sound to make the hair rise
on the scalp and the blood congeal within the
veins. Ellen heard it, and her heart stood still.
It was a groan—the groan of a spirit in heavy
travail, and it died away upon the sweet silence
of nature like the wail of a lost soul consigned
to outer darkness for ever. And, of all the
pains endured by the unhappy girl upon that
never-to-be-forgotten night, the one which left
the most lasting impression upon her mind was
the sound of that groan. Soon afterwards Fox
spoke articulately :

"Hech, how me! but my love is long in
coming to her grave in the cold ground !"

If any doubt still lingered in the girl's mind
as to the identity of the person for whom the
grave had been prepared, these words must
have removed it. Shortly after speaking, Fox
rose to his feet, filled in the unused grave,
shouldered his spade, and strode away. The

dawn was breaking.  But it was long ere Ellen
could succeed in undoing the convulsive grasp
with which her hands had laid hold upon the
tree.   And it was very nearly broad daylight
when a ghostly figure reeled and stumbled upon
the threshold of her father's cottage.

.        .        .        .        .        .

Some months elapsed before Ellen and Fox
were again brought face to face.   Their meeting occurred at a gathering held at the house
of a neighbouring farmer to celebrate the New
Year.   The farm-house was at some distance
from her father's cottage ; and, as the cold was
severe, and the pastoral hill-country swathed in
snow, it was considered somewhat imprudent
for Ellen, whose health had lately been delicate,
to attend the party.   But she was bent on being
present.   The farm where it was to be held was
the very one upon which Fox had last been
employed ; and, if he were still in the country,
she might be pretty sure of meeting him.

An abundance of lights, a few evergreen
decorations, healthy faces, and simple merriment made the scene in the barn, where the
party took place, a cheerful one when Ellen
entered.   Her arrival, however (unlike what
would once have been the case), added little or
nothing to the gaiety of the scene.   Within the
last few months a marked change had come
over her.   And to-night she looked pale, and

seemed to wish to avoid notice or conversation, so that the alteration in her became the subject of comment and speculation.  The proceedings of the evening were to be inaugurated with feasting ; then the tables were to be cleared away, and dancing was to commence.  During supper, Ellen sat beside her father, scarcely either tasting food or raising her eyes from the table.  Yet, though she did not raise her eyes, she was doubtless well aware of the fact when Fox, entering late, accepted a vacant seat which was offered him facing her own, but further down the board.  When the eating and drinking were at length over, speeches and toasts followed, and songs were in demand.  Now, Ellen was known throughout the country-side as a sweet and powerful singer ; but, owing to the depression from which she was obviously suffering, it was scarcely expected that she would allow herself to be prevailed upon to sing that night. So that it was a pleasant surprise when, after a very little pressing, she consented to give them a song.  On rising to her feet, she was received with applause ; then, putting aside the eager call for this or the other old favourite, she struck up a ditty which was new to all present. In the simplest rhyme, set to an old ballad air, she began :

"The other night, as I sat high,
   Waiting for one who should pass by, . . ."

and went on to describe how a tryst had been set between herself and the man to whom her troth was plighted; how the meeting-place was a wood; how she arrived first upon the scene, and climbed into a tree.  The interest of the company was aroused, as well by the novelty of the story and the forcible manner of the telling, as by the beauty and charm of the singer.  She then went on to describe how her lover next appeared, bearing the spade; and how she watched him unseen from her tree.  And, as she reached this portion of the story, her singing attained to an intensity which acted visibly upon the audience.  Every head was bent towards the singer, every eye fixed upon her; and such was the stillness that, but for the music, a pin might have been heard to fall.  It was now observed that, as she sang, Ellen's beautiful eyes, filled with an expression of heart-broken reproach, were fixed upon the eyes of a man seated opposite to her—who, fascinated, returned the gaze.  She sang on.  And ever as she sang she rose to a yet higher pitch of tragic passion.  At last she pronounced these words :

"My limbs did quiver, the leaves did shake—
I saw the hole *the fox* did make. . . ."

At that moment there was a commotion in the barn.  Uttering words which were not clearly intelligible, a man rose excitedly to his feet;

and at the same moment the singing abruptly ceased. The singer—like some nightingale who has surpassed herself in melody and shall sing no more—had sunk back into her seat. The nerves had been strained to the utmost, and with the rising of Fox, Ellen's self-control had given way. There was a general rise, followed by confusion and crowding, and it was some minutes before the convulsed form of the girl could be borne from the barn. In the meantime, Fox had disappeared. Nor was he ever again seen or heard of in that district.

What had been the motive of his intended crime? Was it resentment at some act of lightness or coquetry on the part of Ellen? Was it that strange, fatalistic, causeless jealousy, often read of in newspapers, which seeks by death to secure the loved object once and for all? Was it the madness of some frightful form of abnormal passion? These questions history does not answer. But the tree whose friendly shelter was the means of saving Ellen's life may still be seen by any curious visitor to the sweet pastoral vale of Bowmont Water.

# A MATCH NOT MADE IN HEAVEN.

## I.

LATE on a June night, a good many years ago, Lizbeth, the orphan niece and house-mate of the Minister of Hownam, left her uncle's Manse clandestinely. After pausing for a moment to make sure that there was no one stirring, she raised her skirt over her head so as to form an improvised hood, and tripped forward with a beating heart toward the garden gate. Whither was she bound so late? By all the laws of probability, as a Lowland Scottish maiden, she ought to have been on her way to keep a tryst. But Lizbeth was unlike other girls; she had never had a lover, and she was not bound to meet one now. Her surreptitious nocturnal errand had another object—one which appealed to the feelings less, to the imagination more.

At the period of which I write, charms by the aid of which, at stated seasons, a girl might predict her " fate " had by no means fallen into disuse among the Scottish country-folk. On the contrary, at that day it would have been difficult

to find a peasant-girl who had not, at some time
or other, put to the test the virtues of hemp-
sowing, the toasting of nuts, the watching of the
" droukit sark-sleeve," or some other of those
many spells—so strangely mingling laughter
and terror—which were supposed to enable her
to pry into the secrets of the future. Thus it
happened that, an hour or two before we first
see her, Lizbeth had baked over the dying
embers of the kitchen fire, and then eaten, a
little cake, in which the chief ingredient was the
first egg laid by a young fowl. She had then
retired to her bedroom without breaking silence.
But, as we have already seen, she had not
remained there, but had stolen forth again as
soon as the house was hushed in sleep. The
fact was that the most important part of her
elaborate spell remained yet to be put in practice.
And this was a part which would make no small
demand upon her courage and powers of action.

But before having recourse to supernatural
assistance, Lizbeth had first some distance to
travel. The garden gate closed noiselessly
behind her, and as it did so a slight shiver
passed over the girl's sensitive frame. It was
produced in part by the cool night air, in part by
fear. But the feeling from which it mainly took
its character was that sense of dissipation which
Nature, for some reason of her own, has made
sweet to a certain type of woman,—the excite-

ment so dearly delightful in early youth of doing
something new, bold, dangerous, and—wrong.

The Manse of Hownam lay at the extremity
of the hamlet. The country immediately to
the westward—a valley lying in the midst of
a wide hill-region—is green and open, shaggy
with broom and gorse, intersected by rivulets
and by the river Kale. Once clear of her prison
—for as such the perverse girl chose to regard
it—Lizbeth's slender form sped along so rapidly
and so lightly that it almost seemed as if borne
upon the wind. The long summer twilight of a
northern latitude still prevailed over the darkness; and as the maiden tripped onward over
the tufted green, her floating shape, in its white
summer draperies, might have passed for a
painter's fancy of a Gossamer Queen. Yet
could some stern and masterful adventurer, as
in the fairy-tales of old, have laid hold upon this
seeming-intangible shape and compelled it to
look him in the eyes, the impression would
rather have been that of some Feu-Follet,
Melusine, or other sprite of incarnate tricksiness
and mischief. The form, indeed, was the very
perfection of lissom and tenuous girlhood and
virginity, just touching upon womanhood. The
little face was perfect, too, in contour and in
colour. But in expression it was a surprise.
There perfection, satisfaction, ceased; and
material for reflection, tending ever more and

more to doubt, to hesitation, was supplied.   It might have been likened to the expression of a face without a soul, or perhaps, more precisely, with a soul as yet unborn.   I have seen it almost exactly reproduced in a design of Fuseli.

The girl still flitted on.   Once when, in passing by a patch of woodland, a motion of the air brought to her nostrils the rich mingled scent of meadowsweet and other midsummer flowers, of wild thyme hidden in the herbage, and of blossoming trees, she paused, threw back her head and closed her eyes—drinking in with delight the heavy natural incense-fumes which made her senses reel.   Evidently, if the soul were, indeed, as yet unborn, the senses at least were awakened and alert.

She hastened on.   At last her course took an upward direction—she had begun to climb a hill. Its summit was her destination—the spot which had recommended itself to her imagination as the ideal scene in which to greet the rising moon, and seek her mystic aid.   On reaching it, she sank breathless and exhausted to the ground. The moonrise was not yet.

The grassy, skyward, hill-top upon which she reclined, waiting, presented two features of interest.   They were both of them the work of man's hand, but their respective dates were separated by many centuries.   The first was a cairn, or tall conical pile of loose stones, such as

hill-shepherds—"for a bit of fancy," as one of
them once expressed it to the writer—are partial
to erecting. This monument crowned the apex of
the hill, and it was upon a detached stone beneath
its shelter that the truant maiden crouched.
The second product of man's handiwork was a
circular earthwork, pronounced by antiquarians
to be a British camp, which ran round, and
enclosed, the upland. Within this cincture, a
flock of the hill sheep, whose instinct of safety
leads them to seek the high ground for night
quarters, lay huddled and scattered. Thus
environed Lizbeth sat, with eyes fixed upon the
sky-line at a point, toward the east, where it had
already begun to grow silvery.

I have stated that Elizabeth Bellendean had
never had a lover. But is there any reader who
will suppose that her present nocturnal escapade
had been entered upon in the pure spirit of
disinterested divination? Certainly not. In
coming to the lonely hill-top, unaccompanied,
by night, in the hope of confronting the
simulacrum of her future husband, Miss Bellendean had, perhaps unconsciously, the thought
of a certain person in her mind. Though she
had never had a lover, and had never been in
love, yet she had once had a trifling adventure
(if it may be dignified with the name) which—
thanks partly to the monotonous life she was
compelled to lead, partly to her own imaginative

temperament—had made a deeper impression upon her than would have been supposed. The thing had happened thus. During her solitary walk one afternoon in the previous autumn, she had been disturbed in her reverie by the near approach along the road of briskly-moving horse's hoofs. She had looked up and had beheld—not one of the neighbouring farmers, or their sons, whom she knew and despised —but a handsome scarlet-coated sportsman, mounted on a tall chestnut horse. Lit by the silver sunlight of late autumn, the warmth and magnitude of the vision had somehow struck the fanciful girl with a sense of power and splendour. But this was not all. After glanc-ing in her direction, the horseman had drawn rein, and making some explanation about a delay—a lost shoe—had inquired if the hunt had passed that way.

The girl could give no information in answer to the questions put to her; but, at the moment when the sportsman was about to pursue his way, he had turned in the saddle, and speaking with the ardent gallantry of an older day— which was, nevertheless, without offence, such honest admiration did it betray—had cried, as if the words came from him in spite of himself: " I know not who you may be; and as for me, I have lived a sworn bachelor till this hour. But, if you will but say the word and mount

behind me, I'll make you my wife at Coldstream
Bridge to-night!" (The last words were an
allusion to the "border marriages," still much
resorted to by eager couples in those days.) On
hearing them, Lizbeth had turned with a shrill
mocking laugh, and run off in an opposite
direction; whilst the horseman, with an ejacula-
tion, the purport of which she did not hear, had
cracked his hunting-whip, and had been quickly
lost to view. His too impulsive declaration had
received a rebuff which probably produced a
reaction in his feelings. Yet, could he have
guessed the effect which, soon and late, his words
were to exercise, he would have had no cause to
be downcast. In the months which followed,
Elizabeth, in her dreaming leisure, had returned
to them again and again. For her they had come
to mean not merely one ill-considered speech of
gallantry, but the revelation of the power of her
beauty, the vision of a romantic courtship, a high-
born match, another life. For some time afterwards she had looked to see the red man again.
Perhaps, she thought, she would see him again;
perhaps he would come again. He did not come
again. In her secret heart she was disappointed.
It is true that it was, to a large extent, as a
symbol that he possessed interest in her eyes;
yet the fact remained that it was in the scarcely-
defined hope of seeing the scarlet-coated cavalier
again that the girl had come to the hill-top

to-night. And did she then really believe that, through the moon's intervention, she was going to meet anybody at all? Not for one moment, she would have answered, had the question been put to her directly. Acts, however, are apt to express our minds more deeply and more sincerely than words. And she was here.

## II.

THE rim of the young moon rose slowly above the dark confronting hill-range. By slow degrees the lone still summer world grew lighter, and grey clouds and ghosts of distant hills began to be revealed. As the first fire of the moon appeared over the hill, the girl rose from the ground. Bowing and bending her willowy form in the most profound and reverent of curtsies, she then first made thrice obeisance to the emerging witch-queen of the night, the goddess of her adoration. Next—stepping featly, her head poised, a hand at either side still slightly raising her skirts—she began to trip to and fro upon the green, threading, as it seemed, the mazes of some mystic and intricate measure. Dancing thus unseen, the woman was fairer to look upon than Bathsheba. Her youth, her airiness, her grace, her very soullessness, made themselves each portion of the dance. The primeval, natural joy in rhythmic motion, untouched by any after-thought of coquetry or of "effect,"

inspired her steps.   The "poetry of motion"
stood revealed.   And, as she danced, she
crooned to herself a low, wild, plaintive melody.
Meantime the moon was steadily mounting into
view; and as it rose, a shadow sprung into life
behind the girl, and, elf-like, aped her move-
ments.   The moonlight flooded the valley, the
body of the planet became detached above the
hill, and the dance grew more impassioned,—the
maiden crossed her feet, dipt, whirled, stept this
way and stept that, more delicately, more daintily,
more dexterously, more swiftly than before.
She had let go her skirts, and her waving arms
passed hither and thither, aloft and alow.   Her
voice, too, rose—vibrating slightly on the stillness, and the fateful words of the spell became for
the first time audible.   They were as follows :—

> " *New moon, new moon, I hail thee,*
> *This night my true love for to see;*
> *Not in his best or worst array,*
> *But his apparel for every day;*
> *That I to-morrow may him ken*
> *From among all other men!*"

The tones of the girl's voice died away, and
she sank exhausted at the base of the cairn.   A
modern thinker who had witnessed her perform-
ance would have cried aloud that Paganism was
not dead, but had been lurking in unseen corners
all these centuries, to come forth alive and bold
to-night.

Upon the close of the dance, there succeeded an interval of suspense. The girl's breast heaved, her eyes were dilated and gazed in front of her. The moon, like a solitary ship in a calm blue sea, sailed up the sky. Then, with the lapse of time, insidiously, the sense of travesty, of mockery, began to infect and to jar upon the high-wrought emotions of a few moments before. Certainly it was well to call spirits from the vasty deep, but a query most pertinent and to the point was, would they come? On this occasion it seemed that they would not. Still the girl waited on, the tide of her feelings rapidly subsiding from its exaltation to an ordinary every-day level which was pitiful and painful by contrast. At last, at last, it seemed quite useless to wait any longer, and with an exclamation of bitter self-mockery, Lizbeth rose to turn away. Her foot was now as heavy as it had before been light, and all the life and buoyancy seemed gone out of her. The moon, from her lofty station, looked down with disdain on her foiled votaress.

So, at least, to Lizbeth's sickened fancy it at that moment appeared. The next moment she started violently and shrunk close within the shelter of the cairn. And, indeed, a sudden change had taken place in her surroundings which might well have startled more placid nerves than hers. By an instantaneous transition, impossible to account for, the summit of the hill—till now so lone and still—was visited by animation—nay, by panic and confusion. A sound of many hurrying feet was heard, and the flock of sheep, which had hitherto lain motionless and senseless, swept past across the enclosure. The rumour of their flight passed away; but, as it did so, another sound fell distinct upon the listener's ear. It was that of a footstep, advancing slowly over the summer-hardened surface of the hill. Who walked so late? Had she looked for the appearance of Death in person, the girl could scarcely have awaited it with a more agonised intensity of reluctant expectation. A man's form detached itself from the outline of the cairn and appeared at some distance, walking upon the earthwork and relieved against the sky. Lizbeth's eyes were fixed upon it.

Now, a moderate degree of mental excitement gives intensity to impressions; an immoderate degree tends to obscure and render them uncertain. And so, in the present instance, the tumult of her feelings, combining with the distance and the half-light, obscured the senses of the watcher, blurring her vision. One thing, however, she instinctively noted—the figure wore a sable, not a gala, costume, appearing, indeed, to be attired in mourner's garb. It stalked onward until it had traversed about a fourth part of the circle of the Camp, and had thus come directly opposite the girl; and then, pausing for a moment, and seeming to her eyes to waver against the sky, it vanished into air. Then, and not till then, as by degrees she began to recover herself, did Lizbeth take account of her impressions.   And in so doing, to her dismay she discovered that she had failed in her prime object of seizing the details of the phantom's appearance.   She might meet him again by the light of day, and fail to recognise him.   Bitterly, then, did she reproach herself for her faint-heartedness; but cudgel her brain as she might, she could not coerce it to show her what was not there.   Only she retained an impression that the figure's gait was pensive, and that its features, when for a moment the moonlight fell upon them, seemed pale.

Well, she had accomplished her errand.   Almost beyond her dearest hopes, her prayer had been granted—she had had the opportunity for which she had craved.   But she had failed to use it.   There was nothing now to be done but to go home again.   Gathering herself together, she arose, and crossing the enclosure, mounted upon the earthwork.   As she stood there for a moment, her heart bounded in her bosom. Far below her, on the moonlit hillside, she had descried once more the sable phantom of her vision.   Its apparent supernatural vanishing was

thus explained into the simple act of stepping
down from the barrier on the outer side.  The
figure was descending the hill and passing from
her.  The girl, who but a short time before—
when it had approached her—had recoiled from
it with loathing, now started in eager pursuit
of it.  And so, down the moonlit steep, passed
the dark shape—be it of sleepless shepherd
or night-wandering ghost,—the white, dancing
figure of the lady flitting after.

The ground, which was stony and broken,
retarded Lizbeth's progress.  Nevertheless, in
the course of a few minutes, the distance which
had at first separated her from the object of her
pursuit had been materially lessened.  Then her
advance became more circumspect,—she carefully kept her distance, and availed herself of
the chance cover afforded by a stunted thorn-
bush, or a jutting rock.  Meantime the apparition moved on steadily, without once turning
its head.  In this manner they had approached
the foot of the hill, when the male figure turned
aside and entered a little sunken rocky glen.
With due caution Lizbeth followed.  Progress
was now more laborious than ever.  A stream
flowed through the centre of the glen, and the
footing in the wet and stony bottom was
difficult for a girl.  The figure, however, still
moved steadily on, and for some time, as she
followed the irregular zig-zags of the glen,

Lizbeth managed to keep it intermittently in view. But the light was by this time waning, and at last she lost sight of it for a longer time than usual. Stumbling, wetting her feet, tearing her dress, she struggled on desperately down the uneven descent, hoping in spite of hope that the next turning would disclose the figure to her view once more. It was in vain—somehow or other the phantom had eluded her. At last, weary, wet, bruised and distressed, she emerged from the glen into a valley, where the rivulet joined a river. It was now almost dark, yet she strained her eyes eagerly to right and left. No trace of the figure she had followed so fondly and so long was anywhere to be seen. Her "fate," the one man in the world whose destiny was bound up with her own, had passed away from her, his features undisclosed. Then she sank down, in her drenched white dress, on the cold ground, and sobbed as if her heart would break. And at last, beside herself in the wild paroxysm of her sorrow, she lifted up her voice, and cried aloud into the night, "Oh, my love! my love! come to me—come to me!" There was no answer; but just then the moon went out. The girl was left alone in the darkness.

It is a man's part to love substance; a woman's weaker nature may fall enamoured of a shadow.

## III.

FROM that day a marked change began to be observable in Lizbeth Bellendean. She grew more listless even than heretofore, more perversely indifferent to all that, in the household in which she lived, was held right and proper. Her old uncle, the Minister—a kind-hearted man, and something of a *savant* in his way— was yet one of those born bachelors who never can, by any effort of the mind, understand the nature either of a woman or a child. With the best intentions in the world he had begun, in her callow youth, by spoiling his niece; and now—when she was grown so far beyond his comprehension and control—he could think of nothing better than to leave her to her own whimsies. In other words, he benevolently neglected her. The only other inmate of the Manse was an aged female servant named Kirsty—with whom Miss Bellendean did, on all occasions, precisely what she chose.

The old woman was Lizbeth's confidante; and to her she would often now address herself —entering the kitchen at nightfall—in this wild, inconsequent fashion:

"Oh, Kirsty! I feel so depressed to-night— I declare I long for death."

Then the shocked crone would murmur kind conventional expostulations, which fell unheeded

on her charge's averted ear. Lizbeth's attention
was directed inward, not outward, and a moment
later she would exclaim :

" What would I not give to be going to a ball
to-night ! Lights, music, delicious movement,
admiration,—those are the things I was born
for. I shall die *here*."

And then she would throw her arms round the
old woman's neck, and give way to tears.

She also contracted the habit of taking long
solitary walks. In the morning she would start
forth, fresh, cheerful, hopeful—as though she
were going to meet some one; and in the
evening she would return drooping, despondent,
tragic, as after some cruel disappointment, or
separation. And yet she had not spoken to
a soul all day. Then she would sit for hours
together by her window—alone, unoccupied, as
if she were waiting—waiting for somebody to
arrive. Of course nobody came ; and then her
tearful, unconquerable, lowness of spirits was
piteous to behold. What, meantime, was the
internal travail of her mind, only herself could
have made known.

In course of time her health became affected,
and she had to give up her long walks. Then
she passed into another phase of the crisis, or
climacteric, of her life. She grew weaker ; and
the bright, lovely colour in her cheek gave place
to a chlorotic pallor. She seemed to be falling

14

into a decline. In an older time, she would have been said to be bewitched. Then the anguish of her depression left her, and she discovered a soothing pleasure in sadness's very self. She would now talk to Kirsty—in low plaintive tones and with a wan smile on her face—of the prospect of her life being a short one, seeming, indeed, to be even more than "half in love with easeful death." The fears of the foolish old faithful attendant were aroused ; and deeply distressed, she took counsel with the well-meaning, but sand-blind and helpless, Minister, insisting that some steps should be taken before it was too late. Thus it was agreed between the old people that Lizbeth must have a change of air, and should be sent to the seaside.

The girl herself was very unwilling to leave home ; but, strange to say, she was now more docile than she had ever been before. (This, indeed, was deemed by Kirsty one of the most alarming symptoms of the illness.) Accordingly, on a fair day in autumn, Lizbeth was removed by a succession of conveyances to the nearest sea-port, distant a long day's journey. There her abode was the house of an elderly gentle-woman in narrow circumstances, who was a relative of the Minister's. Neither the hostess, the house, nor the sea-port town—which was, in fact, little more than a fishing-village—was at all to Lizbeth's taste ; and she had not been a

week in her new quarters before she wrote to
her uncle, declaring that, far from feeling better
in health, she felt much worse since she had
come to the seaside, and further urgently
requesting him to come at once and fetch her
home again.  As she had already explored the
village and found nothing there to interest but a
good deal to repel her, whilst awaiting a reply
to her letter, she remained secluded indoors,
refusing obstinately to inhale the invigorating
sea-breeze.  It so happened, however, that a
chance remark let fall by her hostess supplied
the needed vital stimulus in place of the sea-
air.

One afternoon, the two women were seated
together, working with their needles, when the
younger chanced to make some enquiries of her
companion concerning a certain stately mansion-
house, which stood by itself, and dominated the
village from the other side of the harbour.

"That," replied the elderly maiden, "is the
dower-house of the Deloraine family; but it
is better known hereabouts by the name of
Gallantry Hall."  And, as she pronounced the
name, she smiled a withered smile.

"What a queer name!" said Lizbeth.

"Ay, it is a queer name; and a queer story has
been told of how the house came to bear it.
However—whatever may have happened in
times gone by—no gallantry goes on in the

house now, that is certain; for no woman is ever permitted to pass the threshold."

"Indeed! And why is that?"

"Because the present owner is a recluse, who, having suffered a loss, or disappointment, in early life, has forsworn the society of women."

"How romantic! I suppose he's an old man?"

"Quite the reverse—not more than six or seven and twenty." Lizbeth was silent; but, after a pause, she spoke again to ask how the recluse spent his time, and in whose company.

"In that of the fishermen of the village, sometimes," replied her informant, "but mostly alone, and in fishing and shooting, and in wandering far and wide through the country, as I am told, generally by night."

Lizbeth asked no more questions; but somehow her interest in life began to revive. By a process of feminine argument impossible to follow, she had arrived at a belief that the misogynist of Gallantry Hall was the man who had appeared to her on the hill-top. And, if this were so, he was her "fate."

## IV.

ABOUT this time Miss Bellendean's airings were resumed. Her hostess, as in duty bound, would offer to accompany her when she went out; but these offers the younger woman generally declined, on the ground that she was unwilling to derange her kinswoman's habits. Also, when, a few days later, a letter arrived from the Minister, in which he begged his niece for her own sake to give the air of the fishing-village a few days' further trial, she dutifully replied that, since it was his wish, she would do so.

Having already examined the village, she now made the exploration of its environs the object of her walks; but there was a single region toward which her footsteps were never turned. This was the neighbourhood of the dower-house; and so consistent was her avoidance of it, that, had a close observer followed her movements, he could scarcely have failed to be impressed by it. Then—if, in addition to being a close observer, he were also a student of human nature and a reasoner—he might possibly have made the remark that there are two ways in which a woman may betray the direction in which her thoughts lie. The first and obvious way is by recurring to it. The second is by avoiding it. And possibly the saying which declares a certain relation to subsist between depth and stillness in water is of application here. Be this as it may, certain it is that, across the harbour, and more often from the quieter and more distant points of vantage afforded by the heights surrounding the town, the lovely and no longer soulless eyes of

Lizbeth Bellendean often rested upon "Gallantry Hall." The stately architectural façade of the mansion remained inscrutable; but on one occasion, towards nightfall, the watcher beheld a male form come forth upon the balustraded terrace which overhung the harbour. On another, she saw a gentleman with attendants land from a boat at the foot of the water-stairs leading from the dower-house. In both cases she was too far off to observe anything distinctly, yet she pleased herself by establishing a fancied resemblance between the master of the Hall and the figure of her vision on the hill-top. This remote and fanciful communion —if communion it could be called—with one whose fate (as she had come to believe) was closely linked with her own would have been to many women quite meaningless. But, somehow, it exactly suited Lizbeth; and though, as will presently be seen, she was doomed— I write the word advisedly—to experience many emotions more intense and more enthralling, it was to these days that she oftenest in after times looked back as to the happiest of her life. This phase of her life, however, was not destined to be of long duration. It was brought to its abrupt and final close by the incident of an afternoon's walk.

Whilst Lizbeth still lingered on by the sea-side, with the ostensible object of trying the

effect of the air upon her health, the leaves of
the elm-trees in the neighbouring woods had
turned yellow and begun to fall, whilst the blue
mists of autumn veiled the distance.   But the
weather still continued mild.   It happened one
afternoon that, having gone out late after a day
spent indoors, the young lady had ascended
to the ridge of the sloping ground which
rose behind the town.   There, as the shades
of night were beginning to fall, she sat down
to rest.   Her seat, upon a low dry-stone wall
at the roadside, commanded a view of the little
smoky town at her feet and of the sullen sea
beyond.   The air was perfectly still.   The sun
had set, and the boding splendours of a red
after-glow, subdued by on-coming night, were
fading from the sky.   Presently a shower of
cold rain fell noiselessly.   But Lizbeth, yielding
to the enervating influences of her mood and of
the season, still sat on.   Then, from the inland
quarter, a flight of strong-winged birds swept
up and passed overhead.   They flew with out-
stretched necks, and from the symmetrical order
of their flight the girl recognised them for wild
geese.   They were flying, before the approach
of winter and rough weather, to some sunnier
and more genial clime.   As she gazed upon
them, a longing for something—she knew not
what, only that it seemed hopelessly out of
reach—arose in the girl's breast.   The tears

sprung to her eyes; and, her emotion finding
vent in words, she murmured aloud:

" Happy birds! my heart goes with you."

Just then, against the background of the
fading sky, a horseman came into view over the
ridge. His horse was ambling gently. It passed
the spot where the girl was seated, and, the next
moment, setting its hoof on one of the loose
stones with which the road was strewn, it
stumbled and fell. Almost immediately it rose
again; but the rider, who had been thrown, lay
motionless in the road. Springing forward to
his assistance, Lizbeth recognised—by what
means she knew not—the master of Gallantry
Hall. He lay before her, pale and still. She
knelt down, and raised his head in her lap. Still
he gave no sign. There was no assistance, no
water, near; she could do nothing more to
befriend him. And, in her terror, she believed
that he was dying. Then, out of her very help-
lessness, a sharp pang of pity for him and for
herself shot through her heart. Of a surety, fate
had dealt too hardly by them. It had kept her
and this man—who was her happiness, whose
happiness she was—apart till now; and it was
in the moment of death that they now met. In
an access of grief and tenderness, she clasped
the body of the unconscious man in her arms
and pressed her lips to his brow. A few
moments later his eyes opened. Lizbeth then

anxiously enquired if he were much hurt. He
answered no, and proceeded to rise to his feet,
expressing solicitude for the horse's injuries
rather than for his own. But, when the horse's
knees—one of which was cut—had been examined, it was found that the rider's right arm was
powerless. The horse had to be led home ; and,
though with the turn which events had taken a
violent reaction had set in in Miss Bellendean's
feelings, and she would now have given the world
to be anywhere but where she was, yet she
could scarcely refuse her assistance to the suffering horseman. Besides, she felt pretty satisfied in
her mind that he could know nothing of her ill-
judged demonstration of feeling ; which already
—now that she viewed it in the common light
of everyday life—seemed to herself even more
inconceivable than it could possibly have seemed
to him. The two, therefore, walked side by side
but in silence to the foot of the hill ; when,
assuring her that he could now make his way
home unaided, Mr. Deloraine (for it was no
other) wished Lizbeth good-night, and went his
way.

V.

COSPATRICK DELORAINE was the child of his
century. His was the age of Werther and Jean-
Jacques, of Chateaubriand and Lord Byron.
Born to the inheritance of an ancient name, and
of wide and beautiful estates in the Border

Country, he had been brought up by a widowed
aunt with her son, a boy of his own age. The
lads received their schooling from a Scotch tutor,
of humble origin, but of no mediocre attainments.
In their ample play-time they ran wild. They
were, like other country-bred boys, lovers of the
open air, fond of animals, and devoted to riding,
boating, and field sports. Both of the lads were
lairds; and, as they occupied each other's houses
in turn, they enjoyed opportunities of pursuing
every variety of sport afforded by one of the
richest sporting countries in the kingdom. As
regards companionship, they saw less of those
who were their equals in station than of the
peasantry; for it so happened that there were few
boys of their own age among the sons of the
neighbouring gentry. The nature of their tastes
left them much in the care of an old and trusted
gamekeeper—I wish no boy a better mentor;
whilst their admiration of some special art,
quality, or prowess, would lead to their choosing
as their favourite associate, now some farmer's
son, now some working-man or his son, on the
estate. As the lads were both of them gentlemen
born, they lost nothing by such comradeship.

In this manner boyhood sped away, and the
cousins grew up to the rights and responsibilities
of manhood. Neither of them entered a profes-
sion. Cospatrick, when he came of age, settled
down on his own property and led the life of a

country gentleman.  At that time he mixed freely in the society of the county, and before a year had passed over his head it was announced that he was engaged to be married.  The lady was young, beautiful, well-born, highly accomplished, and of a singularly sweet disposition, and all seemed to promise fairly for the future of the happy couple.  Alas! the young lady carried in her system the seeds of a consumption, inherited from a mother as beautiful and scarcely less ill-fated.  When the wedding-day was close at hand, the rupture of a blood-vessel necessitated its postponement.  This was in autumn; at the bridegroom's earnest desire, the new date was fixed early in spring.  But, with the coming of the first snowdrops, the bride was attired for a religious ceremony which was not that of the altar; and the maiden flower which should have strewn her path was laid instead upon her coffin.

Cospatrick was inconsolable.  The brighter half of his own life seemed to die with his betrothed.  Even in childhood, and during his healthy and happy boyhood, he had been noticed as subject to strange fits of taciturnity and depression; and the part of his temperament which these fits had represented seemed now to have absorbed the rest.  He withdrew himself entirely from all general society, and seemed even to avoid the companionship of his most intimate friends.  Much sympathy for him was felt among the neighbouring gentry; however, nobody supposed but that with time his grief would spend itself, and that the lapse of a year, or possibly two, would see him rally, and perhaps even form some new and less ill-starred connection. This showed that Cospatrick's nature had been misjudged. Six months, a year, two years went past and found him still leading his life in sorrow and in recollection.

Soon after the death of his intended, he had given up residing at Brig End—the beautiful seat of his family, situated in Teviotdale—the sight of which seemed to have become hateful in his eyes; and from that time he had lived chiefly at the old Dower House by the sea-port in the Merse. There, with few or no associates but his boatmen and his gamekeeper, he lived a life which—though no doubt intensely real to himself at the time—seems to have left almost no trace behind it. Few traces, at least, have rewarded the careful search made by the writer, a kinsman and successor of his hero. Deloraine (or Delorne, to write the name as it is generally pronounced) had been brought up in the traditions of the country gentleman, and a good deal of his time seems, as a matter of course, to have been spent in field sports. A pack of otter hounds afforded him occupation during the summer months. He hunted the badger by

moonlight on the Black Hill, and shot the blue
rock pigeon from his boat in the sea caves
of the coast.   In the hard winter weather, he
lay, attired in white, in a punt painted the same
colour, on the look-out for wild-fowl off Holy
Island.   These, and such as these, are the facts
to be gathered from jottings in his journals.
But did all his time pass in such pursuits, one
would   wish   to   know?    Did   he   do   nothing
more?    What,   too,   was   the   nature   of   his
thoughts during all these, the best years of his
life?    I   am   at   a   loss   to   say.    Indeed,   had   a
biographer   desired   to   write   Cospatrick's   life,
he   must   perforce   have   been   content   to   pass
over   this   chapter   in   it   almost   in   silence.    All
that can be stated with any certainty is that his
thoughts were of a sombre colour.   He indulged
his grief, and abused the dangerous luxury of
solitude.    Strange   morbid   fancies,   too,   must
have been harboured by him,—at least if all be
true that is reported of his avoidance of female
society, of his nocturnal rambles, and the like.
There was in those days a strange and subtle
spiritual malady abroad, the ravages of which
were felt by some of the finest minds of the
early years of the century.   I am inclined to
believe that, with the lapse of time and with
indulgence, Cospatrick's sorrow became merged
in this distemper.   And thus we may imagine
him, a "mute inglorious" Byron, a Chateau-

briand without the genius, communing with the rainy skies, the sullen seas, the rough-haired cliff-heads and the cruel reefs of the Berwickshire coast in some spiritual dialect of his own, which has passed away, leaving no trace behind it.

Such was the state of my hero's mind at the time when Fate willed that his path in life should intersect with that of Elizabeth Bellendean.

Cospatrick returned home after the meeting thinking only of the accident and of his horse, and the evening was passed in getting his own injuries and those of the animal attended to. Then he retired to rest. But the pain in his wrist and the howling of the wind, which had risen at nightfall, kept him from falling asleep. At last his eyes closed—only to open again almost immediately. But, in the brief return to unconsciousness and in the waking which followed it, certain dimly-perceived sensations of his momentary swoon after the fall—sensations of which at the time he had taken no account—had been reproduced in his brain. The tender enfolding by soft arms, the pressure of kind lips upon his brow, were felt again between sleeping and waking; and as they were felt again as fancies, so they dawned upon his mind as facts. The recollection disturbed him strangely. Who could the girl have been

whose pity and interest had thus so unaccount-
ably mastered her natural reserve?   He recalled
her features as they had appeared to him in the
twilight; he recalled her voice, and the maidenly
grace of her behaviour.   All were alike unknown.
Who could she be? he asked himself again, for
the twentieth time; and how came she, like an
angel of compassion, to have been at hand to
befriend him in the moment of his need?
Wearied with vain speculation, at last he closed
his eyes again; but the recollection of the loving
kiss, of the tender clasping against that soft
woman's bosom, stole back upon his idle fancy
with an insistency which grew to be a torment.
He became feverish, and starting up from the
bed he began to pace the dim-lit chamber and
to think.   The wind blew piercingly without.
As he approached the window in his walk, he
suddenly stopped, and drawing the heavy curtain
aside, looked out upon the night.   The moon,
near the full, rode high in the heavens and shone
brightly, lighting the edges of the white wind-
driven clouds and the whiter foam of the
breaking waves.   Across the harbour the village
lay asleep.   And somewhere, beneath one of
those crowded roofs, sleeping the pure sleep
of maidenhood, there lay one who bore a
heart that loved him.   Cospatrick leaned his
forehead against the window-pane; the tide of
feeling rose in his bosom, and a soft dew

mounted to his eyes—strangers to tears for
many a long and weary day.

The next three days were days of enforced
idleness. On the fourth day, having ascertained
Elizabeth's identity, and having also failed to
encounter her in any of his walks in the streets
of the village or upon the quay—for she was
now keeping indoors again—Cospatrick put on
his hat and sallied forth, bent on satisfying the
demands of politeness by thanking Miss Bellendean for coming to his assistance after the
accident.

## VI.

IT is not my purpose here to describe in detail
the progress of the acquaintance of Cospatrick
and Elizabeth. Suffice it to state that their first
interview was followed, in close succession, by
others. Having once taken the important step
of freely seeking a woman's society, Cospatrick
was not long in discovering that he had made
one of those immense miscalculations to which,
in judging of its own immediate affairs, poor
humanity is so lamentably (or so ludicrously)
subject. He had lived for several years in the
firm belief that love, for him, was a thing of the
past. Instead of that, he now found that, until
he met Elizabeth, it had been a thing of the
future. Keenly susceptible to the charm of
womanhood, as he was by nature, his long self-
imposed seclusion from feminine society had had

the unlooked-for result of making him as
inflammable as tinder. Lizbeth's beauty, and
the charm of essential womanliness so characteristic of her, might well have impressed a far less
impressionable man in far less exceptional
circumstances. As it was, Cospatrick fell at
once the easiest of victims. And, for a man of
his temperament, perhaps the best and brightest
moments in the whole of love are those in which
he says to himself, This is the woman I would
win, and receives the first half-doubtful tokens
of her sympathy.

One evening the lovers had met by appointment as usual. Love does not measure time by
days and weeks ; but, according to the calendar,
only a very short time had elapsed since they had
become acquainted. Cospatrick was melancholy.

"This happiness seems almost too great to
last," he exclaimed, when they had exchanged
greetings. "Its very perfection makes me afraid
of Fate, dearest. Ah, Lizbeth! until I met you,
Fate had no terrors for me ; but now I have,
indeed, given 'hostages to fortune.'"

The girl smiled a sweet, undecided, dreamy
smile, but answered nothing.

"I am haunted by a dread," continued the
young man earnestly, "a dread that something
will come between us even now, to prevent our
ever belonging wholly to each other. I would
give the world to be married to you to-night,

15

dear, even though we were to part at the church door."

"That is quite impossible," answered Lizbeth, smiling gently once more.

"No, it is not impossible—if only you are willing."

"What do you mean?"

"Why, you have heard of Border Marriages? They are perfectly legal. We are within a few miles of the Border now. At Lamberton Toll we might be known and recognised, which would be undesirable; but there is Coldstream Bridge. . . ."

At the mention of the place a sudden change passed over Lizbeth's countenance. The name recalled a trifling incident, now buried (as it seemed) with her past life, and never likely to be disinterred.

"What a wild thought!" she exclaimed, recovering herself quickly, and speaking hastily and lightly. "But, in sober seriousness, Cospatrick, your fears are groundless. We are both of us young, both in good health."

"True. But, Lizbeth, it is a fact that all of my family for many generations have died early, and most of them suddenly. Think if death were to come between us now."

There was an accent of conviction in the young man's voice which had its due effect upon the girl.

When they met again, next evening, he resumed his persuasions. His seriousness, his air of fatalism, and the ardour of his wooing gained upon his sweetheart; and, in brief, she at last consented to drive with him to Cold-stream Bridge the next night to be married there.

For the better understanding of our story, a word may here be said in passing on the subject of Border Marriages generally.   As is well known, they had been first instituted for the benefit of runaway couples from England who might desire to enjoy the advantage of the simpler marriage-laws holding good in the neighbouring country.   For their convenience, a succession of marriage-stations, extending from Gretna Green on the west to Lamberton on the east, had come to be established along the Border line.   For a series of interesting stories relating to the hasty, and more or less informal, but perfectly valid and binding contracts known as Border Marriages, the reader is referred to a scarce little book entitled *The Gretna Green Memoirs*, written by Robert Elliot, the Gretna Green "Parson" of his day.   But, at the time of which I write, the Border Marriage had come to be resorted to as often by persons residing on the Scotch side the Border, and within easy distance of it, as by fugitives from England. Easiness, swiftness, economy, secrecy, and other like inducements were the attractions held out by this lay form of union; and though the contracting parties might as a matter of fact have been united anywhere upon Scotch ground with equal ease, the circumstance that persons ready and accustomed to perform the ceremony were to be found at their stations upon the Border line sufficed to give a preference to those particular localities. Out of this preference a belief seems to have sprung up that the Border line was the only place in which such marriages could properly be solemnised. These unions were naturally viewed with disfavour by the Church; and the Minutes of Border Kirk Sessions during the latter half of the last and the earlier years of the present century abound in records of couples being cited to "compear" before those august assemblies, in order to undergo rebuke for irregularity of this kind. A decent old labouring man who until recently did occasional work for the author was probably one of the last persons married at Birgham by the "blacksmith"—so called, as it appears, in common with others of his trade, from his readiness to "strike while the iron was hot."

It was to a union of this kind that Lizbeth had allowed herself to be persuaded by Cospatrick. The young couple met by appointment soon after dark. A dog-cart was in waiting; and, having decided to avoid the nearer

Lamberton Toll, where one at least of them was likely to be recognised, they set off to drive by way of Chirnside and Swinton Hill to Coldstream. The night was dark. The roads were miry and deserted. Throughout the long drive the lovers scarcely spoke. Seated side by side as they were—Cospatrick's arm from time to time enfolding his companion, as he replaced the wraps which had slipped back from her shoulders—each was borne away upon a separate tide of feeling, tides which (had they known it) were to end by landing them far apart.

At last the lights of Coldstream appeared in the distance, and soon afterwards Deloraine drew up and alighted before the little inn at the Scotch end of the bridge. But here a disappointment awaited him ; for, in reply to enquiry, he was informed, with no great civility, that Armstrong, the so-entitled blacksmith of the place, having had his licence refused him, had recently moved from the house. Here was an awkward predicament for the lovers ; and, to make matters worse, whilst they were still undecided what to do next, a group of the carters (notoriously rough characters) who in those days crossed the Border in large numbers, issued from the inn and collected around them, freely expressing their interest in the situation. Lizbeth was beginning to show signs of distress and her lover of anger, when the blacksmith, who had got word of the

arrival of clients and was anxious not to lose a
fee, made his appearance on the scene. He was
a big, good-natured, swaggering fellow, whose
countenance told tales of free potations, whilst
his address proclaimed him practised in the
science of banter. He had hastily assumed his
garb of office, consisting of a long black coat
and a white neckcloth. Accustomed as he was to
matrimonial emergencies of every kind, he now
brought his ready wit and acuteness to the
service alike of the lovers and of his own pocket,
with the result that he quickly hit upon a
method by which, notwithstanding the fact of
his having been evicted from his house, he might
still read the marriage-service over the young
couple.

Now Armstrong, it must be known, who ought
to have known better, was one of those who
firmly believed in the virtue of the Border Line
—that is, he held that, in order to be efficacious,
the marriage-service must be read by him on
the precise line which divided the two countries
of England and Scotland. In this belief, the
plan which he now proposed to Cospatrick was
to row out in a boat into the middle of the
Tweed, and have the ceremony performed there.
Cospatrick at once saw the advantage which
would accrue from so doing, in delivering
Elizabeth from the presence of the rough on-
lookers ; and accordingly he approved the plan

A boat used by the proprietor of Lennel House lay close at hand; and without further loss of time the little wedding-party moved towards it. The crowd of carters followed. By this time, their clownish interest was thoroughly aroused, and entering in their own way into the spirit of the proceedings, they had provided themselves with torches such as were used by salmon-leisterers in "burning the water," which they lighted and bore aloft. The bridegroom then assisted the bride into the boat, the blacksmith, an oarsman, and a torch-bearer following. The Tweed, which runs strong and swift round the bend by Coldstream Bridge, was that night running stronger than usual. Nevertheless the boat was shoved off and rowed out into mid-stream; where the oarsman kept it stationary, as for salmon-fishing. And there, under the midnight heaven, with the sough and swirl of the water in their ears and the light of the blown torches fluctuating on their faces, Cospatrick and Elizabeth were made man and wife.*

## VII.

COSPATRICK and Elizabeth spent the first few months of their wedded life in seclusion. This protracted honeymoon, as must be stated, was less of their own seeking than it was due to circumstance. The mansion-house of Brig End

* The marriage in the boat on Tweed is historical.

had stood so long unoccupied as to be, in the judgment of the bridegroom, entirely unfit for the reception of his bride.    And so, during the execution of the necessary refittings and repairs, the newly-married couple—who, for various reasons, did not wish to remain at the Dower House—took up their abode upon a remotely situated estate of Cospatrick's known as The Barony.    The prospect before them, of a winter during which he and his wife were to live entirely to each other, exactly suited Deloraine's inclination.    And, at the present stage of their wedded life, the making of plans of course rested with him.    Later on, as he told himself, there would be plenty of time for his wife to take up her proper position in the society of the county.

. The Barony was an old house, occupying an elevated site, in a hill district.    It stood a little back from a high road, upon a long curving ascent of which its front windows looked out. But this nearness to the public thoroughfare only served to increase the sense of loneliness inspired by the surroundings ; for the passers-by upon the road—sighted always so long before they came to hand—might on any day in the week have been counted by a person posted in the window of the house upon the fingers of one hand.    A few melancholy trees overshadowed the slated roof, and the wide bare landscape

spread round about.  As the crow flies, Lizbeth's new home was not very far distant from
her old one.  But, as there was no road leading
between The Barony and the village, she could
not avail herself much—even supposing that
she wished to do so—of her nearness to her
uncle's manse.

The winter set in wet and windy.  There was
no great cold, and no fall of snow.  But on day
after day the wind blew, driving loose ragged
fragments of rack beneath a hopeless sky;
whilst ever and anon the rain changed to sleet,
and the sleet again to rain.  On such cheerless
mornings, Cospatrick would sometimes breakfast alone, by candle-light; and then, having
taken an affectionate leave of his wife, would
ride away to attend a distant meet of the fox-
hounds.  On these occasions, he would return
again in the gloaming, tired, wet through,
and splashed from head to foot, but delighted
to see his wife again.  And then, after dinner,
he would fall asleep in his arm-chair.  On
days like this, Lizbeth was, therefore, left
practically entirely to herself.  She had no
callers; for the few distant neighbours in that
out-of-the-way part of the country had been
bred in the old-fashioned Scotch belief that,
until a newly-married pair have made their
appearance at public worship in the kirk, it is
not seemly to call upon them.  And so, as the

Deloraines happened not to go to church, no
one came to their house.   But, in her solitude and
idleness, the newly-married woman had plenty
of time to think.   Her resources were now, if
anything, fewer than they had been during her
girlhood, for she had no longer enforced occupa-
tions to help her to get through the time; whilst
she also missed even such small distractions as
the village had afforded.   In these circumstances,
her thoughts, to which she was able to give such
free play, were not long in leading her to the
discovery that married life was not quite what she
had expected it to be.   However, she cheered
herself with the assurance that everything would
be all right when she and her husband went to
reside at Brig End.

But Cospatrick, to do him justice, showed no
great keenness in following the hounds that
winter; so that the newly-married couple spent
by far the most of their days together.   The
weather kept them for the most part prisoners
indoors; but to this Cospatrick did not object.
He was, indeed, head over ears in love with his
wife, and could remain seated with her by the
fire, or wander in and out of the room in which
she sat, and be perfectly happy all the time.
His nature lacking something in balance and
restraint, he was probably now too unreserved
in the expression of his feelings.   He could
scarcely have committed any greater error.   For

—to leave out of count the enervating effect of emotional excess upon the moral fibre—a lover ought always to remember this,—that love, where it is complicated by passion, is the embrace of foemen, for which the prudent warrior does not lay his armour aside.   During all this time, as I need hardly say, Cospatrick's treatment of his wife was kindness' self.   Yet, at the same time, there were certain particulars in which—as, for instance, in his present choice of a residence for her—he betrayed a deplorable incapacity to enter into her tastes and her character.

The winter wore on, and was one of the mildest on record,—the hill farmers in the neighbourhood of The Barony being put to almost no expense for hay for winter keep for their sheep. But, in the month of March—when people had already begun to speak of the winter as past —there came a change.   Chancing, late one evening, to consult the weather-glass, Cospatrick observed that the mercury had fallen to an extraordinarily low point; and, during the night following, there occurred an historical snow-storm which is used as a standard of comparison to this day.   In the surrounding hill-district, hundreds of sheep and more than one human being lost their lives.   Every road was blocked, and communications were cut off, in some instances, for weeks.   Supplies were thus stopped, giving rise in certain places to serious privations; and, in short, many striking incidents occurred, which, under favouring circumstances, may perhaps some day be brought together in one of these tales. Cospatrick and Lizbeth found themselves entirely cut off from the outer world, and for some time impeded from venturing more than a stone's-throw from their door. Fortunately they had plenty of stores and of fuel, with mutton at command. Nevertheless, it was during this period of monotonous and wearying enforced indoor life, that Lizbeth first began clearly to realise that her husband was not in any respect very different from other men. And, with a creature such as she was—the very thistledown of the winds of Circumstance, a being fashioned by nature in the form of woman but denied the supposed essential attribute of moral gravity—this knowledge was of far greater import than it might be to another. No wonder she believed in Fate, for she herself was on Fate's side; she had no spirit of resistance. She had married her husband under the fascination of the romance which clung about him, of his high birth, his melancholy, his passion for herself—attributes which had been idealised by the action of her own imagination. Before their marriage, her knowledge of him was solely such as had been acquired in brief enraptured interviews, during which her lover's passion had inspired him. Now he appeared to her in the common light of every-day life. She saw him, yellow with want of exercise, kicking his heels by the fireside, yawning, giving expression to trite and hackneyed statements and remarks. And, as she looked on the spectacle of reality and contrasted it with the phantom raised by her imagination, she smiled a strange, sibylline, inward smile, and felt a little ashamed when she looked back upon herself as a fascinated being.

At last the ways were opened up, and the snows melted. Then the welcome news arrived that the house of Brig End was in a state of more or less readiness to receive its master and mistress. Lizbeth's spirits instantly rose, and she pushed on the necessary preparations for the change of abode with a practical energy which she certainly did not often display. Cospatrick, on the contrary, showed little eagerness to leave The Barony. "Dearest," said he, speaking rather wistfully, when at last the moment of departure had arrived, "I hope there are many more months in store for us as happy as those we have spent here." "Of course there are," replied Lizbeth, whose quick and delicate sympathies seemed now no longer to answer quite so readily to the tone of her husband's remarks. "Of course there are—and many happier, too, I hope!"

## VIII.

For Lizbeth the true happiness of married life
seemed to begin with her arrival at Brig End.
The term of her residence at The Barony had
been, as she now told herself, a mere untimely
survival of her girlhood.  But now, at last, she
began to taste the pride and pleasure of being a
lady.  On the night of her arrival at her new
home, as she passed through a succession of
stately rooms on her way to partake of a
delicately served repast, she had caught a
glimpse of her own form reflected in a distant
mirror, and had laughed and thrown her arms
impulsively about her husband's neck, in a way
which was very rare with her.  Life, she felt
sure, would be worth living here.  It had been
almost dark when she had arrived; and, on
rising, somewhat late, the next morning, the
first thing she did was to go to the window and
look out.  Extensive stretches of green park-
land met her eye.  They were bathed in
joyous sunlight under a blue sky, bounded by
distant woods, and diversified by fine timber
trees at present just breaking into leaf.
"Mine!" she cried aloud, and clapped her
hands, and then made haste to array herself in
order further to examine and explore her new
possessions.  Her husband, with the indifference
of a man who has been accustomed to these

things all his life, at first scarcely entered into
her naïve delight.   But, having come to understand it, he took a pleasure in ministering to it.
The family jewels, diamonds and sapphires, had
long been put away, but he now brought them
to light, and himself keenly relished the process of trying the effect of the flashing and
sparkling pendants, bands, and stars, which had
already decked so many shapely heads and
lovely throats, upon the neck and brow of their
latest and loveliest heir.   Then he hunted for a
lost key, and unlocking a cupboard in which old
satins, brocades, and laces had been put away,
left Lizbeth to rummage among them as she
pleased.   And so she spent a whole bright afternoon amid old faintly-perfumed woven and
embroidered fabrics and half-opened caskets,
lost in her own delight.

Her earliest attempts in the character of the
great lady gave her no less pleasure.   She
would sweep into the neighbouring town in her
luxurious barouche, which was painted yellow
and drawn by bays with black points, herself
attired in an elegant mantle, and holding aloft
a pretty sunshade.   And, as the heads uncovered
as she went by, she would bow and smile sweetly
in return.   She also did her part by calling at
the principal shops, and giving large orders for
things which she did not require.   For, of course,
no one knows the value of money less than a

person who has never possessed any. She had
naturally that particular sweetness of disposition
which, so long as all goes smoothly, sincerely
finds its greatest pleasure in doing pretty acts of
kindness. So she played the fairy god-mother,
addressing herself to the task, not merely of
captivating, but of winning the hearts of her
humble dependents. She was truly kind and
considerate when she talked with them out of
doors, or visited them in their cottages; she was
infinitely charming, she gave herself no airs.
Pity that she had only such honest and true,
but sadly blunt and inarticulate material, as the
Border peasant to practise all her pretty arts
,upon! They did not understand each other
very well. She was not met by the response
which she had expected, and she soon grew
weary of well-doing.

To play the part of patroness among the shop-
keepers, and of Lady Bountiful among the
peasantry, was very well as a beginning; but
that alone was not enough. Lizbeth had still
to make her *début* among the gentry—that *début*
on which so much depended. The marriage in
the boat had been the talk of nine days in the
county; however, as it was known to be a
perfectly correct, if a somewhat unprecedented,
kind of marriage, the ladies of the neighbourhood
agreed to take the line of laughing at Deloraine's
eccentricity, and accordingly left their cards upon

Lizbeth. Cospatrick, who was a degree or two less ignorant of worldly matters than his wife, was most anxious for her own sake that she should be a success in society. But he naïvely supposed that, with her charm and cleverness, there was little chance of anything else. And so, having given his wife a few well-meant hints (for which, by the way, she did not seem effusively grateful), he accepted an invitation, addressed to his wife and himself, to stay for a few days at a house in the neighbourhood, where a large party was to assemble for a ball.

A perfectly cynical onlooker might at this juncture have seen the promise of an interesting situation, to the issue of which he would no doubt have looked forward with a certain amount of amused anticipation. The Society of the County in question presented no exceptional features; it was no less honourable, and no whit narrower in its sympathies, than that of any other. Lizbeth, on the contrary—whose beauty and whose temperament alone sufficed to constitute her an exception to all rules—was even less sufficiently equipped with knowledge of the world than an ordinary young country-woman in her position might have been. And now, between the normal and the exceptional, between the individual on the one hand and the class on the other—the class to which the individual not only did not belong, but was opposed in her

16

interests, her instincts, and her experience—an
encounter was to take place, and a *modus vivendi*
was to be arrived at. The odds were fearfully
against Lizbeth; the result, indeed, in those days
of exclusiveness on the part of the territorial
aristocracy, might almost have been reckoned
a foregone conclusion. Already there was in
existence a degree of prejudice on the one hand,
of defiance on the other.

"They must take me as God made me," said
Mrs. Deloraine to her husband, when he was
finally admonishing her in the dressing-room
just before they went downstairs. "Surely that
is not asking so very much?" (She glanced
archly at the mirror as she spoke.) "At any
rate, he has not made my nose awry like the
Countess's, or given me a rough skin like Miss
Nepean's."

At the same instant, Miss Mally Dempster,
celebrated for her beauty and her raillery, had
been remarking to her confidential *femme-de-
chambre*—

"I own to a curiosity to see Cospatrick
Deloraine's choice. As a rule, I am no admirer
of your rustic belle, who has generally the
colouring of a penny doll and the deportment
of a drudge carrying a milk-pail, with an arm
thrown out to balance it."

Notwithstanding this, a few minutes later,
when Lizbeth came downstairs, the tables were

at once turned in her favour.   Her exquisite
beauty was presented admirably set off by a
rich, though simple, dress ; and, as she entered
the drawing-room, leaning upon her husband's
arm, a little late, an involuntary murmur of
admiration actually burst from the assembled
guests.   It was one of those occasions on
which spontaneous feeling gets the better of
studied manners, and beats them with their own
weapons on their own ground.   Probably it is
scarcely necessary for me to add that the
murmured homage proceeded principally from
the gentlemen.

As the successive couples defiled into the
dining-room, Lizbeth's beauty was the sole topic
of the remarks which were exchanged.   Of
the judgments passed, those which were not
enthusiastic were coldly favourable ; for public
opinion was at present so strong as to render
anything but adherence imprudent.   Perhaps
the most telling compliment which Lizbeth
received was that which came from Lord St.
Ronan's—an elderly gentleman wearing a blue
ribbon across his breast, who had been a
distinguished public servant, and who now
declared to his neighbour that Mrs. Deloraine
reminded him strikingly of Lady Hamilton,
whom he had known in her best days at
Naples.

So far—if any trust were to be placed in

appearances—the *débutante* had scored a brilliant success. Alas! it was not quite the right sort of success; neither was it fated to last long. In fact, the first of it had been the best. And, indeed, as matters developed themselves, it soon became evident that, in the present contest, Lizbeth's very merits would fight against her. Furthermore, it is undeniable that much that she did—however good in itself—was not good amid present surroundings. And so she began to lose ground. Then, as a matter of course, she was not without her ill-wishers; by whom, ere long, the very comparison with Lady Hamilton had been turned to her disadvantage. In all this she was unfortunate; but it would be unfair to conceal the fact that her conduct also afforded some just openings for criticism— if not, indeed, for actual offence. Of these openings it is needless to add that her enemies made the best use. First of all, she betrayed the proverbial flightiness and perversity of a beauty, to a degree which could only appear altogether admirable in the eyes of men who were in love with her. And of these there were not more than three or four present. Next, when she had begun to feel a little piqued, she so far forgot caution as to indulge her spleen by "quizzing" the personal peculiarities of a respectable, though ungainly, fellow-visitor. This was obviously a mistake. And,

having shocked,—poor girl! she had no better
inspiration than to shock again—to show that
she did not care. The house where she was
staying—the residence of the Member for the
County — was a large one; and the party
assembled in it comprised visitors of various
degrees of social dignity. Lizbeth soon found
herself the centre of an admiring circle of the
least dignified ; and, by the very act of stooping
too generously to such admiration, she began
ere long to discover that she was forfeiting even
that. In her despair she lost her head, and went
from bad to worse.

### IX.

MRS. DELORAINE took her social defeat to
heart far more than she cared to show. That
it had amounted to nothing less than a defeat,
became with time plainer and plainer. Out-
wardly she assumed, in regard to the society of
the county, an artificially heightened demeanour
of indifference and defiance. But whilst—so to
speak—she thus snapt her fingers so bravely, it
required all the time but pitifully little skill of
human nature, or of woman-nature, to discover
the true motives which had led her to pronounce
the grapes sour.

It is not, however, to be supposed that, though
the ladies of the county gave her the cold
shoulder, she had no society at all. The reverse

was the case ; she had plenty. Indeed she had too much, for what she had was of the wrong kind. Wilfully determined to prove to her neighbours that she did not suffer by their neglect, she had applied herself with zeal to the task of entertaining. Among other hospitalities she instituted what in those times was known as an "open day" at Brig End once a week. On that day she made welcome almost every one who could command the tailor's part in respectability. The entertainment provided was of the most lavish description ; and the guests, to give them their due, did not require to be "compelled to come in." In truth they did not belong to the class of people who at a feast need pressing. By these entertainments, and by the fame which they acquired, Lizbeth hoped to convince the persons who held aloof from her that she could do without them. But here again her knowledge of the world was at fault. The class whom she at once defied and fondly hoped to win were never to be allured in this fashion. Her entertainments, instead of improving her position, did her reputation grievous harm. Intemperance was the common vice of those days; and stories of excesses committed at Brig End were circulated through the country. It is more than probable that the greater number of these stories were exaggerations—if not, indeed, actual fabrications ; yet

the weekly promiscuous feast can scarcely have
taken place without sometimes touching on the
orgy.   When Lizbeth saw in what direction
things were tending, she promptly checked the
progress of events.   But she had already done
herself irreparable mischief; and, from being
merely neglected, she now began to be tabooed.
Furthermore, she had unwittingly let loose upon
the world a crowd of enemies, in the persons of
discarded sycophants and parasites.

Cospatrick will probably be blamed for not
having kept his wife from committing these
errors.   But, truth to tell, his influence over her
was now no longer what it had been.   She had
done as she liked all her life, and—now that she
was fairly settled down as a married woman—
she had no intention of doing otherwise.   Her
husband, for his part, was perhaps not altogether
sorry to escape from his own thoughts in the
feverish excitement engendered by the round of
wild entertainments of which his house was now
the scene.   The little, imperceptible "rift within
the lute," which dated from the days spent at
The Barony, had been widening ever since.
Lizbeth, absorbed in other interests, was now no
longer at any great pains to keep up the outward
forms of affection for her husband; whilst he, on
his side, had found himself at last compelled to
abandon his dream of what his married life was
to be.   But, with the steadfastness which was a

part of his rather uninspired nature, he still per-
severingly strove to gather up the fragments of
his shattered ideal, and to make the best of what
remained.    In this self-imposed task his wife
did not lend him much assistance.   She was, in
fact, passing through a phase which is common
in early wedded life,—a phase in which the
woman feels her patience to be severely taxed
by what she fancies to be the particularly trying
peculiarities of her husband's disposition, though
they may be in reality only his not immoderate
share of the imperfections which are common to
all humanity.   Cospatrick's fits of taciturnity and
low spirits had returned, and accordingly his
wife chose to believe that moodiness was the
most irritating of all possible defects in a man.
But had her husband happened to be of an
equable temperament, garrulously given, it is
certain that she would have thought the reverse.
The fact is, she had believed that she was
marrying an ideal man.   There is no ideal man;
and, when she found that she had made a
mistake, she laid the blame on her husband's
shoulders instead of on her own.   Possibly
something of this kind happens to most selfish
women who enter blindfold into that married
state of which the true basis is "altruism."   With
time, Lizbeth's native intelligence and her sense
of justice might have gained the day—compelling
her to admit that it was her husband's misfortune,

not his fault, that he was not the man she had
taken him for.   However, it so happened that
time was not to be allowed to her.

It will be gathered from the above that husband and wife had by this time drifted pretty
far apart.   There is no alienation like that of the
newly-wedded.   But, in the intervals when they
returned to something not too unlike the old
familiar relations, Cospatrick scarcely ever failed
to assure his wife that their life would be much
pleasanter when Sir James Bethune, or Beaton
—the cousin with whom he had been brought
up—returned from abroad.   Sir James had at
this time been absent for many months, on the
Continent,—where, after duly making the grand
tour, he had taken up his residence at Venice.
Now, however, he had been for some time past
expected home.   In due course he arrived.
Cospatrick, when the news reached him, displayed some of the boyish exuberance which
had once been characteristic of him, and lost no
time in summoning his kinsman to Brig End to
make Lizbeth's acquaintance.   A slight ailment
which confined him indoors prevented Bethune
from at once complying with the invitation ; but,
as soon as he was sufficiently recovered, he
agreed to spend a Sunday at Brig End.   The
arrears of a country gentleman's business
which had accumulated during his absence, and
which now called for attention, would, he wrote,

prevent his staying longer. He arrived on the Saturday evening just in time to dress for dinner, and Lizbeth was in the drawing-room, which was crowded with other guests, when her husband brought him up to present him. The words in which Deloraine chose to make the introduction were peculiar.

" Lizbeth," says he, " here is some one whom you know already."

His meaning was that he had spoken so much to his wife about his cousin, that, though she had not seen the latter, he was no stranger to her. But his words were true in another sense as well.

Lizbeth, who had been talking to some one else, turned her head when she heard her husband's remark. Her eye fell upon her new kinsman ; and, as it did so, she felt the shock, though not the pain, of a stab in the heart. The gentleman before her wore a scarlet dress-coat, for the hunting-season had come round once more. And in him Lizbeth instantly recognised the man who had made her the off-hand proposal of marriage on the road near Hownam long before, and who had afterwards filled for a time such a prominent place in her thoughts.

Native aptitude, improved by recent practice, enabled her to mask her confusion pretty successfully, and she said what was appropriate in the appropriate tone of voice. But her

mind was still in a whirl when—dinner being
announced, and there being no gentleman
of higher rank present—she found herself
obliged to ask Sir James to give her his arm.
The situation was decidedly awkward. But, in
a few moments, her confidence began to return.
Sir James's manner was perfect. He made no
overt allusions to their ever having met before,
and he seemed far too fine a gentleman to
attempt to remind her of it by any covert hint.
Presently, as they chatted agreeably together,
she felt quite reassured. Next she felt more
than reassured—she felt convinced that what she
had taken for Sir James's fine acting had not in
reality been acting at all, and that he had indeed
forgotten her. She felt immensely relieved; but,
side by side with the sense of relief, there arose
in her breast a sense of disappointment. When
Monday morning arrived, to Cospatrick's delight,
the baronet consented to prolong his visit.

Sir James Bethune was a man who enjoyed
life. To do this wisely is the triumph of
the philosopher; but Bethune's temper had
certainly nothing philosophical about it. In this
statement no censure is implied. He lived in
that world of impulse, which constitutes, so long
as youth remains, no unbecoming *entourage*.
And his impulses, proceeding from no luke-
warm nature, were generous as often as not.
But it is little better than a truism that the

impulses, even of a wholly generous nature (which his was not), taken at random and uncorrected, are no safe guide through life. They must almost inevitably lead, though by a circuitous path, to the undue aggrandisement of that Self from which they proceed. In person Sir James represented a type of British manhood which, though good, is not uncommon. He was of the middle stature, and stoutly built; with hair and whisker of a light red colour, blue eyes, and sanguine complexion. His distinction, which was undeniable, proceeded not from his appearance, but from a sense which had been born with him, which had grown up with him, and which it would have been ridiculous to obtrude, that he was somebody in the world. In this respect he formed a contrast to his cousin, whose ways and manners, in their natural unpretentiousness, fell far short of the standard which Lizbeth had come to set up. As a young man who had seen something of the world, Sir James had a degree of polish, and possessed a little more than the mere indispensable modicum of reading. Conscious of the shortcomings of his nature on the philosophic side, he had determined to have a philosophy of one kind or another, and, as he was very anxious to be cleverer than he really was, he had selected Voltaire as his master. Among his other favourite writers were Macchiavelli, Rochefou-

cauld, and Chesterfield; whilst he would quote
with great apparent relish the epigrams of the
Marquis de Talleyrand, which were then still
novel. So, before long, his practice began to
conform a little to his preaching. Such a thing
it is to have a philosophy by rule of thumb!
Besides, his prolonged residence in Venice had
done him no good.

When the slight awkwardness of their first
meeting at Brig End was past, Sir James
and Lizbeth became excellent friends. The
baronet spent much of his time at his kinsman's house—which, under the circumstances,
was natural enough—and generally in his kinsman's wife's society. Cospatrick viewed their
intimacy with satisfaction. He felt that, as
a means of keeping Lizbeth entertained, as
she liked to be, he was himself a failure. Sir
James had more conversation, and exerted
himself more in the use of it than his cousin,
who would too often seek to regale his wife with
(for instance) some story without an end about
a horse which somebody had sold to somebody
else. This was a side of her husband's nature
for which Lizbeth had scant tolerance. She
would have liked him always to remain at the
plane to which she had seen him rise unconsciously in moments of emotion, but to which
he had not now risen for many a day.

The two who, as the proverb tells us, are

company, are seldom perfectly loyal to the third
person who is none.   From casual references,
Lizbeth and Sir James got on to little criticisms
of Cospatrick, and to little witticisms at his
expense.  Things had been for some time in
this position when an incident occurred which
served further to precipitate matters.   One day,
after lunching alone together, Mr. and Mrs.
Deloraine had an altercation.   It was not their
first.   It arose out of a trifle, which provocation
soon magnified, and before the matter was
allowed to drop, both husband and wife had
let their feelings carry them away, with the
inevitable result that hasty words were spoken.
Five minutes later, the respective attitudes of the
disputants were eminently illustrative of the
gulf which separated their natures.   Neither, as
yet, acknowledged to having been in the wrong;
but Cospatrick, seated with bowed head by the
hearthstone of his gun-room, took the matter
deeply to heart, whilst muttering to himself
something which was not perfectly intelligible
about "the eternal spirit of unreason incarnate
in a woman."   Lizbeth, at the same moment,
stood before her glass, engaged in tying the
strings of a new bonnet.   Her face was a good
deal flushed and her fingers trembled; but her
countenance expressed a firm determination not
to be brow-beaten, and she had just ordered the
carriage to go for a drive.

On coming downstairs, the first person she encountered, as she crossed the hall on her way to the door, was her cousin by marriage. Sir James had his hat and hunting-whip in his hand, and had just entered the house unannounced, as was his custom—having left off following the hounds early after a blank day. His quick eye immediately observed the disturbance in Mrs. Deloraine's demeanour, and almost as quickly he guessed the cause. He bent forward, and shaking her tenderly by the hand, he murmured —in the presence of the servants, but so as not to be heard by them:

"Ah, what a mistake you made, that day upon the Hownam road!"

The revelation, taken together with the degree of secretiveness, and of strategy, thus brought to light in one usually supposed to be so open and impulsive, had an effect which was little less than startling.

Lizbeth hurried on towards the carriage, without saying anything in reply. But, during the two hours of her solitary drive, the words which had so much affected her had plenty of time to sink into her mind. This little incident was the beginning of a change in the character of the intercourse between Lizbeth and her husband's cousin. The little criticisms of Cospatrick grew to be complaints on the part of Lizbeth of the unhappy life she led with him, and sympathetic

condolences on the part of Bethune—condolences
which at last forced her to believe that she had
more in common with her kinsman than with
her husband.   And, if this were so, was she not
bound to admit the mistake with which the first-
named had taxed her?   Alas! as she now felt,
her insane, superstitious infatuation about her
"fate" had led her grievously astray.   Whether
consciously or unconsciously, the young people
were now treading on dangerous ground.   And
the doctrines of Sir James's favourite philosophers
seemed to come near to playing the part played
by the Story of Sir Launcelot in the Italian
poem.   Meanwhile time was passing, and changes
were taking place, of which no one at the
moment took account.   But these changes were
none the less real in that they were noiseless
and internal.   At last the time arrived when
their results were to be made manifest, and this
is how the manifestation came about.

At that period the wave of military ardour
which had arisen with the expectation of a
French Invasion had not yet entirely subsided.
Almost every gentleman, excepting the aged
and infirm, was a member of some corps or
other.   Cospatrick and his cousin held captains'
commissions in the local regiment of militia.
One night, during the training, it happened that
they were dining together at the mess with
other officers of the corps.   The after-dinner

potations of those days were deep ; and it often happened that, as the night drew on, remarks were not very carefully considered, passions by no means well kept under control. Cospatrick sometimes drank freely, in the hope of removing the depression of spirits under which he suffered. Sir James, on the other hand, not only never exceeded the bounds of prudence in his drinking, but never seemed to lose for a moment the coolness of his head. What actually gave rise to the quarrel which took place was either never clearly known, or, as is more probable, was never divulged. All that is certain is that Deloraine, suddenly, and as seemed to most present, without provocation, insulted his kinsman grossly. Bethune, to do him justice, seems from the evidence led at the trial, to have done his best to avoid a quarrel. But Cospatrick's fury is asserted to have been that of a madman. Failing by mere words to produce the effect he sought, he coolly proceeded to fill his glass from a decanter of claret which stood by, and flung the contents in Bethune's face. This was more than the baronet's equanimity, or possibly than his reputation, would bear.

In those days the duel was still the common court of appeal in disputes of honour between gentlemen ; whilst, at that particular period, the military spirit abroad in the country had given it a special vogue—a vogue which, in such

17

irregular corps as that to which the kinsmen belonged, had tended to become exaggerated. As the militia officers sat at the mess-table, their swords hung on pegs against the wall behind their chairs. And now, with a simultaneous movement, each of the cousins—or foster-brothers, as indeed they were—turned behind him. And to each, as he did so, it seemed the most natural thing in the world. They had been brought up together in brotherly love; but things between them had somehow sadly but completely changed almost without their being aware of it. Swords were crossed. Of the other officers in the mess-room, no one would seem to have attempted serious interference. This was due, no doubt, to the fact that, on the night in question, all who were present happened unfortunately to be very young men, junior in rank to Deloraine and Bethune. The hour, also, was advanced; and the young men may not improbably have reached a frame of mind in which to regard the present playing with edged weapons as an exciting frolic, or a piece of sport on no account to be spoiled. The cousins, who, in happier days, had fenced together times out of number, were known to be evenly matched; and, of course, until it was too late, no one dreamed that serious consequences might follow from the engagement.

But, from the first, the eyes and faces of the

combatants, their desperate lunges and their
eager sword-play, might have told a different
tale.   In the midst of the circle of gay uniforms,
and of foolish flushed boys' faces, they stood
confronting each other like men who have a
long account to settle.   The first few passes
were exchanged without skaith to either; then,
as, after pausing to breathe, they set to again,
an untoward accident occurred.   In pressing
his adversary before him, in a warm attack,
Cospatrick had changed his footing, and he
now stood close upon the spot where a part of
the claret which he had discharged in his kinsman's face had fallen on the floor.   The building
was a rough temporary one, and the new bare
boards of which the floor was composed had not
yet absorbed the moisture.   With his next step
forward, Cospatrick's foot slipt in the puddle,
and he stumbled forward.   As he did so, Sir
James's sword-point caught his breast and
entered his body on the right side.   The wounded
man's sword-point dropped and fell; and, making
a half-turn to the left, he caught the edge of the
mess-table, and stood supporting himself and
coughing.   Then the blood began to drop from
his lips upon the table-cloth, and it was discovered that his antagonist's weapon had passed
through his body.

   He was at once borne to the nearest bed, and
laid upon it.   Medical assistance was at hand,

and his wound was promptly dressed. It was pronounced to be of a most serious nature. Asked if he wished to see his wife, the wounded man replied in the negative. An attendant sat up with him. There was a light burning in the room, by which Deloraine's eyes were seen to be open. The attendant asked him, kindly enough, if he would not like to try to go to sleep. He answered no ; that he was thinking. And so he lay, with open eyes, without speaking, until the morning drew near. Then he called the attendant to his bedside, and dismissed him to bed. The lad was loth to go, but his master's word was law. And, as the door closed, the sick man murmured to himself :

" I have lived alone . . . stretching out my arms in vain into the void. Let me die as I have lived."

When the doctor returned, soon after daybreak, his patient's eyes at last were closed.

Bethune's advisers deemed it expedient that he should fly the country. Accordingly he made all haste to interpose the Channel betwixt himself and the long arm of the Law. But presently, being informed by friends at home that, by the help of the fortunate accident of the spilt claret, a sufficiently good case might be made out for him, he returned and successfully stood his trial. Nor, during the remainder of his life, would he seem to have suffered very much either from

a damaged reputation or from a remorseful
conscience. A stroke of apoplexy carried him
off at the age of sixty.

What of Lizbeth? One last surprise in her
eventful wayward career remains to be communicated. Hurried as had been Sir James Bethune's
departure from England, he had found time
before he left to solicit an interview with the
widow of his kinsman. She declined to receive
him. Nor could she be persuaded to vouchsafe
a more gracious reply to the most eager written
entreaties of the man for whom she had
sacrificed so much. Truth to tell, the terrible
tidings of her husband's violent death had
sufficed to precipitate a reaction, which had
perhaps already been impending—a reaction
of repentance, which was now doomed to be
intensified by all the additional horrors of
remorse. Strange irony of the fate which a
woman creates for herself! Now that she had
lost him for ever, Lizbeth for the first time
appreciated her husband at his true worth. In the
early days of their acquaintance, her attachment
to him had been compounded of almost purely
selfish elements. She had admired in him—
and, to do her justice, she had done so in no
mercenary spirit—the abstract beauties of high
birth and fortune—beauties which must neces-
sarily appeal, in their due degree, to all who
have eyes for beauty in its every manifestation.

His romance and his fatalism had pleased her
fancy.  His overmastering passion for herself
had filled her with a new sense of power.  But
these attractions had long since worn out.  And
it was now that, for the first time, beneath the
superficial qualities, the superficial flaws, of his
character, she recognised the depth and the
truth, the simplicity, the tenderness and  the
kindliness of his nature.  These qualities, I say,
she recognised ; and, recognising them, as was
her wont, she went further and idealised them.
And so,

> " How much I loved him,
> I find out now I've lost him,"

became the burden of her daily song.

And, as it was not in her nature to rest content in thought alone, she adopted a strange
way of life which should give an outward visible
form to her inward mood.  She continued to
live on at Brig End, in a seclusion almost as
profound as that which Deloraine himself had
cultivated in his salad days at Gallantry Hall.
And she vowed to devote her life to carrying
out, in the management of the estate, and in
other like matters, what she believed would have
been her husband's wishes.  But she did more
than this.  Everything that could remind her
of Cospatrick she kept religiously about her.
His dogs and horses became her especial care.

The old servants of whom he had been fond were retained in her service, and in due time were comfortably pensioned, and required to work no more.   Among these there was one old man whose sole duty she made it to clean Cospatrick's guns, to polish his boots, and to lay out daily in the hall his cloak, his hat, and his gloves, just as if it were likely that he would need them again.   The old man did his duty faithfully ; but in due course he died.   By this time the boots had gone to pieces ; but now— kind reader, must I acknowledge it ?—the old tattered cloak, which still remained, was allowed to drop from its peg in the hall, like a ripe fruit from the tree.   Was Cospatrick, then, at last forgotten ?   Lizbeth lived on ; and in every Eden into which Eve has penetrated, she lives, moves, and has her being to this day.

# A DEATH-BED VIGIL.

*(Leaves from an Autobiographical Fragment.)*

## 1830.

. . . My life has long since fallen into the " sere and yellow leaf." Love and joy—the birds and flowers of its spring and summer—have forsaken it to return no more. My neighbours pronounce me a misanthrope. What then? is there not that, in my past life, which might well destroy a man's faith in human nature—making him to doubt the truth of woman, to query the honour of his own sex?

Love came to me late in life. I was an only son; but relations between myself and my father had been strained. He was not an affectionate parent; I, on my side, was not the son I should have been. My youth was spent in travel and adventure, in field-sports and sea-faring; and it was not until after I had succeeded to the estate that I took up my abode at Harbottle. The old house stands high upon the steep slopes which ascend to one of the wildest

and most remote of the moorland districts of
Northumberland.   I had not been long at home
when I first saw Phillis Gray.   She was the
daughter of a small farmer upon my own wide,
but poor, property.   But she had nothing of
the rusticity of her station.   The girl was
beautiful, and I loved her at first sight.

The Hedleys of Harbottle are too old, too
proud, and too self-willed a race to trouble their
heads as to how the world may please to view
their alliances, or to suffer such trifles as class-
distinctions to obstruct the gratification of their
wishes.   Miss Gray became my betrothed.
Even at that time I did not flatter myself that
she returned my passion.   I was a plain man ;
I had never cultivated the art of winning
woman's favour, and was no adept in courtship.
But I loved Phillis, not alone blindly and with
the passion of a first and only love, but with a
deep and true affection also.   I did not suppose
that the persuasions of her relatives, the position
I had it in my power to offer her, counted for
nothing when she consented to be my wife.
But that pressure had been put upon her I
never dreamed until too late.   I believed that
love would follow marriage.   I see now that I
took this too much as a matter of course.

As the day fixed for our wedding drew near,
I observed a change in my betrothed.   Impas-
sive, undemonstrative, as she always was, she

had never shunned me hitherto; but it struck me that she did so now. She was melancholy, too; and once or twice gave way to sudden bursts of tears in my presence. I paid little attention to all this at the time, attributing it to the mere natural vapourishness of the feminine character. At last, one night when I was about to take my leave of her, the girl, who had been very depressed throughout the evening, surprised me by asking my forgiveness. I made sure that it was one of her odd fancies. "Forgiveness, darling!" I exclaimed with a laugh, "why, what on earth have I to forgive?" Her reply was made in a tone which, had I not been infatuated, must have struck me as ominous in its solemnity. "Not much," she said, "not much, perhaps, at present—though more even now than you suspect. But some day . . . ere long . . . I may happen to stand greatly in need of your forgiveness. Will you not—to please me—grant it me in advance?" "With all my heart," I answered lightly, and without a moment's hesitation. And then I kissed her and took my leave. I was not long left in the dark as to the motive which had prompted her strange petition. That night Phillis secretly left her home and disappeared. We sought her high and low; no trace of her was brought to light. But, when seven months had elapsed, her corpse was discovered floating upon one of the dark pools below the moors. I looked upon that sweet face, cold in death, which I had loved in life and should mourn for evermore. Suffering had strangely altered it, but this was not all; for, as I gazed on the lifeless form, I recognised that which turned my grief into a sense of wrong, more bitter a thousandfold to bear than the cruel and eternal separation of life and death. My bride that would have been had been betrayed. Gladly would I then have given what remained to me of life to know the name of the villain who had beguiled her innocence, and had wrought this grievous offence against me. But the dead girl was as true to her false lover as she had been false to me. She kept her secret. From that day I lived an altered man.

Two years had passed. One autumn afternoon I was standing, listless and alone, at a window which looked out on to the park. The day had been fine, and the sun was still shining; but overhead a vast and gloomy continent of cloud was moving up from the west. If appearances were to be trusted, we should have rain, perhaps thunder, before night. Meantime busy airs were searching restlessly among the upper boughs of the old trees, turning up the livid underside of the foliage, now in this place, now in that. A little grey bird, too, flying unnaturally high, looked white against the sombre, threatening, heaven. From looking upward, my eye travelled down over the steep green slopes before me, through which the grey rock broke, over which the grey boulders lay scattered. All at once, over the little bridge which spanned the river, far far down, I saw a procession pass. Four men, moving slowly, were bearing something between them. Others followed, some on horseback, some on foot. But for the fact that most of the men wore scarlet, the *cortège* would have had the appearance of a funeral. I saw it for a moment, and then, almost immediately, the nature of the ground concealed it from my view again. I rubbed my eyes. I had lived so long low-spirited and alone, that I was half inclined to believe that the whole show had been a mirage —the creation of my brooding brain,—or possibly even that it had been one of those prophetic visions which are held by the country-folk to portend death.

A moment later and the whole thing was explained. There came a ring at the door-bell, and Jack Selby, booted and spurred and wearing his hunt coat, stood before me. His cheery face was unnaturally grave ; and he informed me, in few words, that there had been an accident in the hunting-field, and that the injured man was being brought to my house. I enquired who the sufferer was.

"You will be sorry to hear, Tom—it is young Binny Clennel."

"But he's not seriously hurt, I hope?"

Jack made no reply, but shook his head very gravely.

"How did it happen?"

"His horse—the young chestnut that he bought from Hodgeon—struck the top bar of a post-and-rails and rolled on him."

By this time horses' hoofs were already heard on the gravel before the door, and voices in the hall. I went downstairs; and there, only too surely, amid the throng of the huntsmen, some on horseback, some dismounted, I recognised Clennel. His hair was wet, his face was pale; he was unconscious, and was borne upon a gate upon which some coats had been laid. Poor boy! Only that morning he had scampered past me in the park—the very picture of ideal youth and manhood, rejoicing in its strength,— and as he passed me, capping the hounds along on to the scent, he had waved to me and shouted, "You should be with us, Tom!" He was my friend.

We carried him carefully upstairs, and made him as comfortable as we could. Then, there being nothing more that we could do for him until the doctor should arrive, I went downstairs again to give the fellows something to drink. We were still in the dining-room, talking over the accident, when Dr. Handyside arrived. A glance at the patient told him—what, indeed, we had surmised already—that the case was hopeless. The spine was fractured, and the injured man might linger for at most a day or two. He was also suffering from a severe concussion of the brain, and he remained unconscious. After giving us directions for treating the patient during the night, the Doctor (who could do no more, and whose attendance was urgently needed by a lady at some distance) was compelled to take his departure,—which he did after promising to return as early as might be next day. His back was scarcely turned, when the members of the hunt began also, one by one, to excuse themselves upon one ground or another, and to take their leave. There was an evident desire on their part—for which I could not blame them—to shake off the gloomy associations which oppressed them whilst they remained in the neighbourhood of the injured man. At last I found myself left alone with Francis Hodgeon, a kinsman of poor Clennel's.

How we got thro' the evening I don't know, for neither of us had the heart to talk, or to settle to any occupation. At last the night drew on, and we began to make preparations for spending it in sitting up with the sick man. I had left Hodgeon in the sick-room, and had gone to the cellar to fetch some old brandy. I

suppose I was away longer than I had intended
to be. At any rate, when I returned, Frank was
standing in the passage, outside the bedroom
door, which was ajar. He seemed much relieved
by my re-appearance ; and as I drew nearer,
I saw that the big broad-shouldered man was
blubbering like a child.

"I can't stand it, Hedley, indeed I can't.
Poor Binny, poor chap! who would have
thought of this ? "

I saw at once that, whatever Frank's nerve
might be in the hunting-field, it was not of the
kind to allow him to be of service in a sick-
room ; so, putting aside a few feeble protesta-
tions which he made, I dismissed him to bed,
and myself prepared to spend the night alone
with the dying man.

When I entered the bedroom, Clennel's condition continued unchanged. Only once so far,
at the moment when we were laying him in the
bed—roused perhaps by the movement, he had
appeared to regain consciousness, and even to
recognise his surroundings. For the room was
familiar to him, being the same which he had
been used to occupy in former days, when a
frequent visitor at Harbottle. At that time
he and I had been close friends. Indeed, so
reserved was my nature that I may say that,
of all my neighbours, he was the only one with
whom I had ever really been on terms of perfect

confidence and affectionate intimacy.  Doubtless
my affection for him was the stronger upon that
account.   And probably, too, the friendship was
most on my side ; for he was happy, and therefore popular, and had many friends.   For the
only people whom we really love are those who
are happier than ourselves.   In any case, no
younger brother could have coiled himself more
closely round an elder's heart than Binny had
coiled himself round mine.   But, excepting
sorrow, nothing in this world remains unchanged ; and thus, after the shattering of my
hopes, a gradual estrangement had somehow
seemed to spring up between us.   We had
had no shadow of a disagreement; but Clennel, by degrees, had ceased to frequent my
house.   I could not wonder at it; for, in my
altered mood, I was certainly no suitable companion for a man of his joyous and ardent
nature.   His companionship might, indeed,
have helped to cheer my gloom ; but as I had
no wish to trammel him with the fetters of
friendship, I had acquiesced in his secession, and
we had ended by scarcely seeing each other
at all.

Yet, as I looked on him now—lying in one
hour struck down in the full flush and hey-day
of his manhood—I knew from the keenness of
my grief that my old affection for him still lived
unaltered in my heart.   His beauty—'tis the

only word—seemed as yet untouched by the
approach of death. Where his shirt had come
unfastened, appeared the wide, virile, chest of
a Meleager. The massive throat, the features
broadly and simply moulded, the well-built-up
brow, had lost none of their apparent grace,—
though I knew that one half of the body was
already paralysed, and that the spirit animating
that fair clay now slumbered—in all likelihood
to wake no more on earth. So, as I gazed
on this masterpiece of Nature's handiwork, so
rudely marred and broken, the cry of Othello
rose involuntarily to my lips. But there were
pains other than the mourner's to be endured
before the night was done.

After moistening the lips of the unconscious
man with a few drops of brandy, I trimmed the
solitary shaded lamp, which, by shedding a dim
light over the heavy, dark, old-fashioned furniture of the room, and by half-revealing its outlines,
served to stimulate the imagination with a sug-
gestion of things unseen. I then returned to
my seat. The room and the house were now as
still as death. But not so the world without.
Neither rain, nor thunder, as I had expected,
had arrived in the wake of the vast clouds which
I had watched at eventide; but, toward the
darkening, the wind had risen, and it was now
blowing boisterously. The old ash-trees round
the house increased the turmoil by the resistance

18

which they offered; and, now and then, a gust of
air from without found its way, by some slit or
cranny, into the lofty chamber where I sat, and
stirred the dusky hangings. My head sunk
upon my breast. I listened to the shrieking of
the wind outside, and fell into a dark train of
thought.

Presently my eyelids must have closed. My
thoughts wandered. The incidents of the day
were strangely blended with fantastic imagery
of the night; and the solid realities of the
Biddlestone Hunt became merged in vividly-
seen, rapidly-changing visions of a Wild Huntsman passing on the wind, of Gabriel Hounds,
and at last—as the howling without grew more
persistent—of a cry of fiends let loose from hell.

Out of this somnolent condition I was startled
by a sound which came from the bed. The sick
man had spoken inarticulately. Gathering my
scattered wits as best I might, I returned to the
bedside, and bending over him addressed him
softly by name. His eyes opened, and for a
moment I felt almost sure that he recognised
me. But it was for a moment only. When that
was past, it became obvious that his unconsciousness was as blank as before. As I bent over
him, however, I became aware that a change
had taken place in his physical condition. A
faint flush had overspread his face, and his
temperature was mounting rapidly. Against

our expectation, a reaction had set in, and an inflammatory process had begun. A moment later he startled me by suddenly flinging his right arm across the bed. Then he began again to speak without words.

I endeavoured to soothe him by the touch and by the voice. I applied vinegar and water to his brow from a bowl which stood by the bed-head. It was to no purpose—he still rambled on. At last, in despair of quieting him, I returned to my place in another part of the room. The minutes then crept by with leaden feet, whilst I still listened to the weary, incomprehensible, interminable, harangue.

All at once, I was sensible that a change had come over the spirit of the sick man's ravings. He had begun to speak intelligibly. The words fell suddenly and in quick succession from his lips, like the first pattering drops of a shower.

". . . Did I startle you ? Ha, ha ! pray don't be afraid—it's only me. I am riding in your direction—I'll see you home if you'll let me. The road *is* lonesome. . . . Well ! to tell the honest truth, I'd a notion you would pass this way."

The voice of the delirious man was rich and expressive as of old. In his present circumstances, there was a terrible irony in the lightness and gaiety of the tones in which he spoke. I noticed, also, that those tones were modulated to the particular soft pitch used by men who are "impressionable" when they address a pretty woman. I was surprised to hear my own name next.

"Hedley . . . ? Ah! what a lucky fellow he is! And he doesn't know his luck,—that's the bitter part of it. 'Tis a matter of course to him. God knows there are some men who would bear themselves right differently in his shoes. . . . Well, well! what's that to me? But it *is* something to me!" (The last words were pronounced with extraordinary warmth and petulance. Binny's widowed mother had spoiled him. Ah, how well I knew the accent of the spoiled boy!) Then the speaker broke off abruptly, and continued, "There, there! I've said too much. Forgive me. Good-night, good-bye. God bless you!"

In any other circumstances, the monologue to which I was now called upon to listen would have been nothing less than a dramatic treat. The tones of the speaker's voice were animated, expressive, "to the life," to a degree which positively astounded me. Thus the blessing had been spoken in accents of such strange and winning tenderness, as I could fancy might well seem music to a listening woman's ear. They were accents which, as it struck me now, my own voice had never acquired. However, I was more than merely astounded by the vivacity of the declamation. It was evident that the sick man was living over again in his delirium some tender episode of his past life. I felt interested more than I can say in what I heard. Was I taking a dishonourable advantage in listening? Perhaps I was. I was dimly conscious of scruples on this ground at the time. But, without staying to analyse my sensations, being desirous—I scarce knew why—not to miss a word, I drew nearer to the bed. There was a pause, which was filled in by the shrieking of the wind. Why had such a feeling of impatience to hear more arisen within my breast? Well, I had not long to wait.

"Oh, 'tis a cruel fate, if ever there was one, and I pity you from my soul! Love, marriage,— they are either the best things on earth, or the direst woe. There's no third alternative."

This time the speaker's words were pregnant and oracular. I had never known him to hold forth in this strain before. Then he grew incoherent again. Straining my ear so as to lose nothing, I vainly strove to put a meaning to the sounds he uttered. But they were absolutely unintelligible; and at last, my patience being wearied out, I sank back into my seat once more. Hardly had I done so, however, when it became evident that the heaven

of the sick man's mind had partially cleared
again.   He was speaking articulately once more.
We were now, as it seemed, in the midst of a
scene half-reproachful, half-impassioned.

" . . . You asked me not to come here again?
I know you did.   Well, there are not many
things in the world I would not do for you. . . .
My word !   You *do* look pretty to-night.   And,
now you blush, the rose grows pale.   You must
give me that rose, darling—as a remembrance.
I'll keep it—wear it next my heart. . . . Little
hand !   'Tis a-cold ; and mine is fevered.   No, I
will not let it go.   You grudge me all things
—you've no kindness for me at all.   And yet I
am *his* friend."

I started.   Then I listened on.

"There's only one thing in the world I wish—
that you liked me just a little better.   I've no
sister.   My poor mother's gone. . . . No, I'm
sure you don't like me as you say you do.   If
you did, ah, if you did. . . . But that's enough."

In this madness I was beginning to discover
a method with a vengeance.

"One sweet kiss—I won't ask for any more.
The old cold-blooded monster !  why, how is
*he* to know anything about it ?   He'll never
suspect.   Isn't all fair in love and war ?   He
thinks he's conferring an honour by making you
his wife, but I can tell you there are men, his
equals, who would think the other way."

During all this time I had been creeping ever
closer to the bed, till I now sat with my knees
touching it.    And, as I crept closer, so an
appalling suspicion grew ever stronger and
stronger within me.    But, up to this point, suspicion, however powerful, yet lacked confirma-
tion.    The next word confirmed it beyond any
doubt.

"Phillis!"

The name was pronounced in a low, earnest,
tone, the accent of which I shall remember to
my dying day.

"*Phillis!   The one thing that makes life worth
living—will you forfeit it, of your free will, with
your eyes open?*"

So much I heard.    Then a rush of blood
mounted to my brain, I gasped for breath, I
fell forward on the bed.    Instinctively my hands
clutched for Binny's throat.    But, as they touched
him, I remembered.    To all intents and purposes
the man whose life I coveted was already a
dead man.    I was powerless.    I could do
nothing.    Even the bitter consolation of vengeance upon his treachery was denied me.    He
had wrecked my life, and now he mocked
me from the security of the confines of the
grave.    I gathered myself up from the bed once
more, and resumed my sitting posture.    And
then there began for me such an ordeal as few
men, I hope, have been called upon to bear.

With my ears open, my eyes closed, I sat on, and listened to the sick man's ravings. And, so listening, I heard—nay, I *saw*, for I was transported where the bounds of sense no longer confine us,—I saw the girl whom I had worshipped shamefully won from me by the man whom I had called my friend. And I well knew all the time that my ordeal was self-inflicted. I might have closed my ears. There was no reason why I should subject myself to this long-drawn-out, unheard-of, refinement of jealous torture. Why did I do it? Why, indeed? Except that Jealousy is hungry as the grave, self-torturing as the scorpion, and at whatever cost must know the worst.

And, as I sat on and listened, I was conscious that, by an unique refinement of Fate's irony, the treachery of my friend cast its blight not only on the present, but on the supposed-unalterable past,—showing me all of love and friendship that I had ever believed myself to enjoy shrivelled up and turned to dust and ashes, as it were, before my eyes. I realised this, and then—whilst the tempest screamed and clamoured round about us—a strange interchange of character and attributes took place between the healthy and the dying man; for, whilst *I* groaned aloud in a heaviness of spirit worse than death, his light and volatile soul found a singularly gracious and tender tone in which to rehearse once more its bygone happiness. Binny was arranging over again in his dreams the details of his elopement with Phillis.

"Dear one, with what a tragic bitterness you pronounced those words just now! 'I am not afraid of sin, I am only afraid of punishment and of detection.' A woman, every inch of you! Well, I'll tell you how detection, at least, may be avoided. You must dress yourself up as a boy, dear. I'll get you the clothes, and will hide them in the old place, near your father's barn. Then, when you change your dress in the barn, you can make a bundle of your own clothes and bring them with you. . . . A pair of moleskins —ha, ha, ha! But mind you wrap the muffler close about you, for if any one sees how round and smooth that little chin is, our game is up. . . . I will be waiting in the dog-cart at the usual place. We'll pass through Hexham unnoticed at dead of night, and be married at Carlisle in the morning."

So the sick man raved on. But, after this, my senses flagged and grew duller. Worn out with the anguish of the disclosure, the gnawing tortures of a retrospective jealousy, I felt at last that I had heard all that I had any need to hear; and the story of a mock marriage and a desertion was borne in upon me only in vague and general terms. Meantime the wind still howled without, and the night wore on. I

suppose I was exhausted ; for at last, strange,
incredible, as it may seem, I fell into a doze. I
was roused from it by a painful and peculiar
sound. The dying man was drawing his breath
with alarming difficulty. Seizing upon the
readiest means of affording him relief, I started
up and drew back the window-curtains. I must
have slept for some time, for the storm was now
over, and it was later than I should have supposed possible. Indeed, the day had already
broken, and a brilliant sun was in the act of
rising—its level beams striking dazzlingly upon
the rain-drops pendent from the window-frame.
Outside, the ground was strewn with a *débris* of
broken trees. I flung up the sash, and the
sweet morning air invaded the drug-sickened
atmosphere of the room. It revived the dying
man, and he called to me by name. I flew to
his side.

"Tom . . . Tom! Oh! lift me, lift me. . . . I
am choking."

It was the last flicker. I saw that the end
had come ; and I felt that, though to have
raised the patient sooner would have been to
murder him, to do so now would be to ease his
final moments. I lifted him gently in my arms.
Then he breathed more freely, and spoke once
more. I bent down to catch his last words.
But his mind had wandered back to old days.

"Give me my cloak and hat," he said, and

endeavoured to make the motion of wrapping himself up. "I must hap myself warm to-night, for I've a long, long way to ride . . . over the moors, through the storm, alone . . . a long . . . long . . . way. . . ."

The voice failed. Then came a succession of sighing respirations, and the head fell forward. Binny was dead.

An hour later I re-entered the death-chamber, accompanied by Hodgeon. We both looked long on the features of the dead man who had been our friend, and presently Frank spoke.

"How calmly and peacefully he lies there! And, do you observe, Tom, what a happy smile lights up his face? It's like the face of a sleeping child. His life was short; but it was merry. After all, I count him happy. For we may feel assured that he dies at peace with all men, and is gone to a better place—having wrought no evil, having wronged no man."

I said nothing.

## EPILOGUE.

Hoffmann! to you.—My wasted candles wink,
Ere their bright eyne they close. And deep I
    drink—
Crowning with ichor a skull-carven bowl—
To Hoffmann, and his twin fantastic soul,
Death's Jester, whose hyperbole sublime
Shall thrill, with Tamburlaine's, the pulse of
    Time!

Hoffmann, you led a strange and motley crew
Of puppets shaped in wood—I follow you:
To Beddoes is most fittingly address'd
The night-side of my fancy, here express'd;
Churchyards he loved—the gibbet and the pall,
The charnel-house, and midnight funeral.

. . . I hear—unheard by day—the voice of floods;
The ceaseless, low, night-murmur of the woods:
An owl, my fellow-watcher, o'er the park
Sends out her voice—her soul—into the dark.
The book is finish'd, and the ink is dried;
I lay the ink-stand, pen, and scroll aside.
Thou tender-beaming Star, o'er yonder crest!
Now light the darkling author to his rest.

www.ingramcontent.com/pod-product-compliance
Lightning Source LLC
Chambersburg PA
CBHW030936260626
47169CB00002B/498

\* 9 7 8 1 4 3 4 4 2 2 7 9 8 \*